THE MORNING

AFTER

C. J. Wade

THE MORNING AFTER
Copyright © 2017 by C. J. Wade
Published by The Write Wade Publishing Company, LLC

All rights reserved. No part of this publication may be reproduced, stored in a retrieval system, or transmitted in any form or by any means – electronic, mechanical, digital, photocopy, recording, or any other – except for brief quotations in printed reviews, without the prior permission of the publisher. This is a work of fiction. Names, characters, businesses, places, events, and incidents are either the products of the author's imagination or used in a fictitious manner. Any resemblance to actual persons, living or dead, or actual events is purely coincidental.

Cover Photo by C. J. Wade
Back Cover Author Photo by Eric Dejuan Photography

For more information or to book an event, please write:
The Write Wade Publishing Company, LLC, 210 Fieldstown Road, Suite 100, #320, Gardendale, Alabama 35071 or visit our website at www.thewritewade.com.

ISBN-10: 1542348943
ISBN-13: 978-1542348942
Library of Congress Control Number: 2017900544

Father, I am so grateful to be a seed that You've sown on Earth. May this literary bloom make You proud.

To my parents, Mom & Pop, I love and appreciate you. We always make a great team because you always let God be the Captain. Your lives inspire me to live. Thank you for letting me fly.

***

This book is dedicated in memory of
Nancy T. Stricklin
artist, author, filmmaker, friend

Thank you for the launchpad of belief.

FOREWARD

"The Morning After" is a well-crafted, powerful, amusing and inspiring work of art that should never be confused with a mere book!

Charged with a rich story-line and shockingly real characters who jump off of the pages, C. J. Wade has created a tale filled with profound wisdom, explosive wit and timeless spiritual truths.

I have found my new favorite author and I cannot wait for the sequel!

Ty Scott King
Poet, Rapper, Author, Radio Show Host

PREFACE

This book was created for you.

I am sure of it.

The words that you are about to read were planted in my spirit in 2008. After ten chapters of development, the last trimester of this book came to a halt. No matter how many times I powered on my laptop, found cozy places to write, and planned "finish the book" dates on my calendar, my words had no birthing place. I could not understand how God could start the flow then stop the faucet. Nothing in life felt right and I grew angry and depressed. Finally, in 2015, I attached meaning to this horrific block and my feverish prayers for clarity and wisdom were answered. A friend's death had created a snowball effect and that ice had carved a cave of darkness within my soul. It was dark and lonely, but I lived in that cave among family, friends, and strangers. Once I admitted my pain to the Father, my prayerful cries resulted in a surge of energy to write my heart out.

So, this book is a testament that dreams can evolve and still come true. There is always a morning after midnight. God's Love can reach you wherever you are. The birth, life, death, and resurrection of Jesus Christ is continuous proof of that fact. Not only can it reach you, His Love can save you from yourself. That is what it did for me.

I pray that as you read the following chapters, you will be healed and liberated from your cave. Look around you and notice the walls that have been built by your own hands and by the actions of others. Be honest. Be real. Be vulnerable and walk toward your morning. Although the darkness is familiar and His presence is with you, your purpose needs the Son to grow. Begin your journey to the Morning Star. Dig deeply, open wide, and allow His Love to fill you up and bring you out of your dark place.

I will be waiting for you on the outside. The view is so much better out here.

Peace & God Bless,

CJW

CHAPTER 1

"But, don't you love me?"

"Of course I do. That's why I'm doing this."

"That's why you're leaving me," Elyse reiterated softly, looking into his eyes with the hopes that her heartbreak would make him re-think his actions.

"That's why I'm leaving *us*, not you. I need to leave all of *this*," he answered, throwing looks of disgust around the great room of their four-story home. "I just can't do it anymore. I can't keep pretending that we're making this work, that we're having this wonderful life. I'm tired of faking this fantasy for you, Lys. I love you, but I'm not *in* love with you anymore. I'm just not."

Kin remembered his Alaskan souvenir on the mantel, a translucent replica of Mount McKinley. Coldly passing to the right of her disbelieving face, he walked over to the mantel and grabbed the frosty piece of crystal. After walking back in front of her, he stooped down to unzip his luxury suitcase and placed the souvenir under the clothing inside. Then, he exhaled deeply.

"You got to believe that this hurts me, too," said Kin, rising from the floor.

Catching the teary lump in her throat, Elyse gazed down at the floor with her hands resting thumbs-down on the small of her back. Most days, she didn't believe a word he said. This time, she wished this was the case. Her eyes shifted left and fell upon their British Virgin Islands honeymoon picture, framed in brushed silver and hanging mockingly on the eggshell-colored wall. "I don't know what to believe right now," she said in a small, exhausted voice.

"You will. One day. I'm sure then you'll understand." He reached his left hand to her chin. As he lifted her face, a tear skipped down her right cheek. She looked away in embarrassment, her chin still in his fingers.

"I'm sorry," Kin whispered. He leaned in with his lips intended for hers, as he had done many times before. She locked her lips together with apprehension, anger, and disagreement. She wanted him to stay, not to appease her.

And he had always used his kisses like a pacifier. Sensing no reciprocity, he kissed her gently anyway. He swept his tongue across her bottom lip. Elyse tried to refrain from the buckling knees, increasing heartbeat, and melting sensation in her body. But it wasn't working. She loved him. For six years, they were inseparable, not counting their three-year dating and two-year courtship. He was her gentleman, always dapper and down to earth. That's what she loved about him. Her lips violated her iron will and she engaged in her husband's kiss. Kin glided his fingers from her chin to her right cheek, the same side that hosted the teary culprit that leaked her feelings into his hands. He pulled away slowly and wiped the tear with the back of his finger. His hands were soft. So was she.

"The house is paid for. Stay as long as you need. I'll send my brother and the movers to get the rest of my things." He walked toward the door as she stood there in the same position that he left her, only this time her eyes were open, and so were her ears, just in time to hear the following:

"Goodbye, Elyse."

The door shut with conviction. He had just left. Her legs wanted to run after him like a lioness after prey. But they didn't. She stared at the marble floor again, practically paralyzed. Her thoughts began to float chaotically to the surface of her mind from the bottom of her heart. She felt light-headed, but she couldn't seem to walk in the direction of the couch behind her. So she stood there, motionless as a statue. Then her eyes blinked.

"I can't believe this is happening," her subconscious spoke. She huffed as her frown turned into a shocked grin. "No. This just *happened*. It's…it's over," she said softly, attempting to swallow the stress by speaking slowing to herself. "This is…this is um…." She paused for a quick intake of breath. The thoughts were aspiring to become words as they came to the forefront, as if Kin was still standing in front of her. Her glassy eyes were just like the doors of her home, imprisoning her inside her own shell. Her dizziness overshadowed her logic to sit down and her legs finally gave way. She fell limp, crumbled into a pile of humanity, onto the marble floor, which felt significantly colder than usual.

"God," she whispered to the floor, "I don't know what to do."

"I need..." she began to admit in a pubescent-cracking voice. She could feel the rush of emotions stampeding up her chest. The surge felt like a herd of horses, trampling and strangling her pride in their path. Then, the crippled words began to pour out of her mouth feverishly in desperation.

"I don't know how to deal with this. I can't cry over a man, but...I love..." Tears flooded her eyelids and spilled over the edge to escape. Although she could feel it, she couldn't manage to say it.

"Okay," she whispered. "I build communities for a living. I can handle this mess." She wiped the tears that crept down her nose with the sleeve of her workout shirt. "I am not doing this," she sniffed in denial. "Get it together!"

Hoping she could make the tremors disappear, more tears raced down her cheeks and more words poured from her pain. She couldn't hold it in any longer. Years of anguish topped with the blood from the stab of confusion were determined to be free. Right then. So, she let it out.

"GOD!" she screamed in desperation. The echoes of her plea bounced up the walls. She was breathing heavily and the tears were unstoppable. A foreign feeling. In the effort to regain her center, Elyse did her best to slow her heartbeat.

"In...out...deep breaths...in...out...slower...c'mon...in...out..."

She rose to her knees, but sunk backwards, placing her weight on the back of her legs. Her palms were red and shaking from pounding the Italian marble.

"I don't know what to do. I just don't know how to...to do this. I need...I...I need You to help me. Just, just guide me. Do something, God! Just please do something! *Anything!*"

Elyse suspended her tearful breathing, gazed past reality and flashed back to their wedding day. The white hue of her dress now looked hazy. The flower girls were blurs of innocent beauty. Her husband's smile was there, along with his regal stature. A foggy image, but there nonetheless. Her parents and grandmother beamed with joy at the reality of their little Lysie finally getting married. Then their faces started to droop slowly, then fast, like rain running its fingers down an oil painting. Elyse blinked to regain focus on the images in her mirage. The flower girls, the friends, the groomsmen, the matron-of-honor—they all melted onto the church floor. The portrait's remains fled in uncharted directions underneath the pews.

"I…I thought we would have children together, travel, and work on our goals together." She paused again, and then finally let out another deep breath. "I just thought things would be different, God. Just…" Elyse exhaled, "…better…different…happy." She hadn't prayed past age 10, and while the act seemed foreign, her exposure in this moment seemed natural. Like she was made to be naked before Him.

"Auntie Lys? Whatcha doin' on the floor?" She looked over her right shoulder and saw her 4-year-old niece standing a few feet away in concern, a purple crayon in hand.

"Just praying, Kaye," she answered, wiping her face. The reality of lunchtime and hosting "Auntie Weekend" dawned on her body and mind and she instinctively resumed her role, like a heroine standing up from an earth-shattering blow and a phoenix rising from ashes.

"So what do you want to eat, kid? Pizza or Spaghetti?"

"PEEEEEE-ZZZZAAAAAAA!!!!!" screamed Kaye, jumping up and down in exhilaration.

"Then pizza it is, Ma'am! Go put away your crayons and meet me in the kitchen."

Kaye took off, running around the corner, and carefully trampled up the stairs.

"NO RUNNING, KAYE!" Elyse yelled. A faint 'Yes, Ma'am' breezed down the hall and around the great room corner. Elyse walked into the kitchen, grabbed her purse from the table, and placed her hands on her keys. She stared at the BMW logo. It was her husband's spare key.

What a day off this turned out to be, she thought.

Trying to shake off the encroaching depression, she looked up. "I can do this," she whispered to herself. She tried to nod slightly to reiterate her pep talk, but her head seemed to be full of the truth. She bit her lip. "I can *do* this. I *have* to." The second time was more believable, yet not convincing.

The fast pitter-patter of Kaye's feet began to slow down once she reached the top of the steps and resumed speed as she approached the kitchen.

"I'm ready, Auntie Lys!" Kaye's eyes were so vibrant and sweet, a refreshing twist from the environment her niece had stumbled into just ten minutes ago.

"Me too, Kaye. Let's bust out of here."

"Yeah! Let's buss outta here!" replied Kaye ecstatically, completely unaware of her aunt's euphemistic response.

CHAPTER 2

Elyse arrived at Delilah's happy hour at 5:44 PM. Smooth sounds of jazz, dim lights, comfortable sofas, and drink specials made Delilah's the premier place to unwind after work. It was *the* after-five place to be on a Thursday night in Birmingham, Alabama. A simple eye-coasting and one could spot a handsome man every few feet and a beautiful woman even closer. Elyse squeezed her clutch a little tighter as she skimmed the room. After the week she had had, even her secret fear of sitting alone wasn't going to stop her from enjoying the beautifully buzzing atmosphere.

"Great. No William," she thought in disgust. "I knew he wouldn't show."

"How many, Ma'am?" inquired the hostess.

"One for now. I'll just take a seat at the bar. Thanks," she replied, still looking around in hopes of catching William's hand motioning her to a table.

"Sure, Ma'am. Take the seat of your choice and enjoy your evening."

She tried to hold her confidence at least arm's length as she walked to the bar area. "I hope I don't look desperate," said her subconscious. "I just want to have a good time tonight. No stress. I have enough to keep at bay. And Lord," she petitioned within, "Please, no crazy people and no stupid pick-up lines."

She reached into her purse and checked her cell phone. No William. No anybody, for that matter.

Sigh.

"This should be interesting," she thought facetiously. The snap of her clutch's clasp jarred her senses to the jazz and sultry buzz around her. She turned around to tune into the band's selection. They had just concluded Duke Ellington's *Satin Doll* and transitioned to *Sophisticated Lady*, one of her favorites. Her parents used to dance in the middle of the living room floor to that historical jewel of sonic bliss. She smiled at the beautiful childhood memory, then changed her attention to the bartender.

"Strawberry cocktail, please."

"Allow me. What are you drinking tonight?" a stranger behind her asked.

"I thought I said no crazy people," she thought.

The toes of her four-inch black heels lightly skated across the bottom rim of the barstool. "Strawberry Cocktail," she replied hesitantly, still facing forward. "But that won't be necessary. Thank you for offering."

"What's your name?" asked the gentleman.

"That won't be necessary either," she replied shortly.

"So, where does necessary begin?" he inquired. Her half-smile gave him the permission he was looking for to proceed.

"My name is Dinner if you want it to be," he said, extending his professional hand and flashing a perfect smile, fresh with dimples. She hadn't truly looked at him until then. A pleasant surprise. She couldn't gauge his height, but she could tell that he was shorter than Kin's 6'2" athletic build. It didn't matter. He was too easy on the eyes and the spirit for her to ignore.

"Cute," Elyse replied lightly laughing. "Thank you for offering...Dinner." She extended her hand to shake his. "Elyse."

Realizing his hands were dewed with moisture from his glass; he wiped his hand on the thigh of his pants.

"You know, you could ruin your clothes like that."

He took her hand in his as if to begin a simple handshake. "You do realize that is a minor detail in the grand scheme of this moment," he rhetorically inquired, gently transposing his hand in position to kiss hers. She smiled with a smirk.

"Old-fashioned. I like that. So why are you in this century, again?"

Laughing, he reached for a sip of his drink.

"I'm here to meet a woman named Elyse, but you could very well be an imposter. How do you spell your name?" he asked intently.

"Well, before I do that, how do I know *you're* not the imposter?"

"That's the beauty of this mission. I think you already know I'm real. You have a pretty good sense of people, but you don't trust easily. Between a history of sexism and professional discrimination, you're not in the mood for anything that doesn't yield a return on your investment. Probably a middle child. Always being the mediator, the advocate, the thinker of the family. Am I right?"

"*Where did this guy come from?*" She asked herself, trying not to spit out the recent sip of her cocktail. "*I have to deflect. Quickly.*"

"My instincts tell me that you have a motive. You still haven't shared your name. Care to state it, or you want to keep playing around it?" she asked quickly.

He laughed again and she was entranced by the way it sounded. It was rich like chocolate velvet, yet carefree like summer white linen. Trying not to show her enchantment, she retorted with a question to cover it up.

"Is something humorous, Mr. Dinner?"

Suppressing his laughter and clearing his throat, he replied, "Absolutely."

Elyse put down her cocktail in curiosity, right on top of the cursive capital 'D' embossed on the napkin. "Please continue."

"Well, I find it hard to believe that a woman like you did not also come to Delilah's with a motive, or as I prefer to call it, a mission. You seem to be a woman of intention, not doing many things haphazardly. So, why can't a man like myself come to this place to socialize with no strings, just converse and mingle? Is that not a possibility?"

Without shifting her weight or her eyes, she responded to his question. "You're correct. That is a possibility. A mingling motive and a *sexual* motive, however, are evenly possible at this point. Fifty-fifty. You could possess one or the other, like most of the men in this room."

"So which one do you think I possess?" he asked her, revisiting his drink.

"Honestly, I've disregarded both possibilities. Your suit implies that you're here to unwind before you head home alone. You aren't here to meet with someone. You're here to scout. See what's out there," she replied, pointing to the tables in front of the stage. "You've taken off your tie, but left on your cufflinks. You're not here to impress. Am I right?" Elyse confidently took a sip of her cocktail to let him marinate. "In a nutshell, I think you're just an intellectually employed psycho with a nice smile. Case dismissed."

They both laughed and continued an enriching conversation. They touched on various subjects, people, and goals, never inquiring the other's profession. Time floated along and the exchange was sweeter than the strawberries at the bottom of her cocktail. His name was Malcolm, which seemed to roll easily between her lips. Elyse liked the way it sounded with her voice attached to it. When the pleasantries progressed to his home, he enjoyed the way she exhaled his name in passion. The intertwining of their souls was unintentional, but a welcomed escape from reality. Her mission of forgetting about the workplace was accomplished, at least for the night. Tackling the office in the morning? That was a completely different animal.

***

"So, you just didn't show, huh?" The heat from her glaring eyes made William remember that she beat him up over Oreos in the fourth grade, plus she made him buy her an extra carton of milk for a week. Now she was standing in the doorway of his office as if she was anticipating another chance to repeat history.

"Something came up, Lys," he replied.

"Yeah, sure. Something always does. I don't know why I keep setting myself up with your invitations. 'Ron and I are headed to Delilah's after work. You should join us!'" Elyse mocked, ornamented with his infamous energetic, yet nerdy voice. "'You should really come out, Lys. I'll be there around 5:30 with a table. Call me when you get there.'"

He sighed. "I really was coming, but Rachel called and…"

"Rachel," she intercepted dryly, as she halted her walk to the door and turned around in annoyance.

"Yes, Rachel," he reiterated. "She called and needed me to run an errand."

"Really."

"Yes, really." He picked up the stapler from the right side of his cherry wood desk. "You really shouldn't be so hard on her."

"Hard on her?! Are you serious? The woman controls you with that invisible leash day in and day out," she heatedly whispered, pointing to his cell phone lying innocently in front of his file folder. "'Go here, do this, buy that...' You can't possibly believe that she doesn't know what she's doing."

"She probably does," said William, placing his stapled papers in the file folder and standing up. "But she's my wife. I love her and you need to respect her as such. You're my friend, Lys, and what you think means a lot to me, but it doesn't govern my life." He picked up a stack of invoices and tapped them on his desk.

Elyse bowed her head slightly toward the imaginary plate of humble pie in front of her. She winced a bit and took a small bite of it.

"You're right. She's with you *permanently* now and I need to accept that. I still don't like her, but I *will* respect her place in your life. I'm sorry," she concluded holding out a thumb's up. "On our friendship?"

He smiled. They had always used that phrase as a reminder of their mothers' wishes for them - "friendship over foolishness."

"On our friendship," he answered, holding his thumb up and pressing it against hers. "And I'm sorry for standing you up. I'll call you on the leash next time."

CHAPTER 3

"Just what are you trying to say?"

Shara placed her electric toothbrush in its red toothbrush case. She carefully wiped her mouth with her face cloth as she radiated sincerity from her eyes to his in the bathroom mirror. Placing the case on the side of the vanity, she explained further.

"What I'm saying is people are starting to ask questions about you that I don't want to answer."

"Questions? What kind of *questions*?"

"Questions like 'What does your husband do for a living?' and 'Your husband seems sleepy a lot. Is he okay?'"

"Maybe your people should mind their own business."

"They're not *my* people, Lenn. They're *our* friends and their questions are valid," she replied, shaping her honey-blonde bangs with her fingers.

"Nosy people don't have valid questions. Tell them to stay out of my business and tend to their own." Annoyed, he walked out of the bathroom and into the kitchen.

Shara looked in the mirror one last time before leaving for work. "Sure, whatever," she muttered to herself as she calmly put on her berry-wine lipstick. One final touch of holding spray and her layered hairstyle was perfect and her morning ritual was complete. After giving herself the once-over in the full-length mirror, Shara heard Lenn returning towards the bathroom. They were aggressive steps. She calmly finished checking her clothes. He was just around the bathroom wall and the clip-clap of his dress shoes indicated that he had more to say. As far as she was concerned, she was in control of the conversation and he could rant and rave all he wanted. She had to report to the school in an hour. Being a middle school principal required a certain level of temperament that couldn't be easily altered. After 10 years in the profession, she was a master at it. Lenn appeared in the doorway of the bathroom with Kaye in his arms. Their daughter's attention was focused on the doll in her hands.

"This," he said in a harsh whisper and pointing at Kaye, "is why they should stay the hell out of our lives. You remember that the next time you try to corner me with questions." Kaye, oblivious to her father's hostility, continued to play with the doll's hair with a miniature comb.

"I'll call you at lunch. Have a good day, Sweetie," she responded. Unscathed, she walked around his huffy bubble and retrieved her briefcase from the kitchen chair. Knowing what was coming next, Lenn grudgingly walked behind her.

"Give Mommy a kiss, Kaye!" Kaye reached out her pint-size hands to cup her mother's face. Shara turned around and leaned in for a light peck on the lips. "Mommy loves you."

"I love you, Mommy. Have-goo-day!" she replied bubbly, repeating her mother. Shara smiled at the joy in front of her and returned the well wishes. "I love you too, Daddy." She kissed Lenn on the cheek and proceeded to the door. He fumed underneath his exterior. In an effort to transpose that energy to something positive, he and Kaye travelled downstairs to the playroom. The layer of ice cracked with the sound of his daughter's voice.

"Daddy, will you play Dominoes with me?"

"Sure, Baby. What type of cookies are we playing for this time?"

"Chocolate chip, Daddy! Chocolate chip!"

"Chocolate chip it is. Three and three?"

"Three and Three!!" exclaimed Kaye, referring to their rule of three games and the three-cookie prize.

"Okay, Shortie. Three and three it is. You get the Dominoes and I'll get the juice and cookies."

"Daddy!" she whined. "I'm not a shortie! I'm this big now!" Kaye raised her arm and bent her wrist a few centimeters above her head to indicate that she had grown, shifting her weight from one tip-toe to the other.

"Wow!" Lenn said surprisingly, "You sure are! You must have grown over night. It happened so fast!"

Kaye's smiled beamed with pride. "Yep! Fast! Vrooooom!" she shouted and took off around him and up the stairs.

"I swear that girl is going to run track at somebody's college one day," he spoke softly. "And I know I'm going to pay for this cookie game later."

***

The week would be a challenge, considering that Kin had sent Elyse fresh flowers on Monday's. She never knew what flower it would be, but it was always on Monday's to help jump start her week. A note with his writing and she would immediately think of his cologne and his shoulders. How they seemed to carry away everything that annoyed her in her professional and personal life. His notes were like preventive medicine for Tuesday through Friday. Sometimes they would have a humorous saying like, "Have you used the bathroom yet?" and other times they would host an erotic quip such as, "I can still taste the honey from this morning." And the flowers. The flowers were never the same. Light lavender petunias, bright yellow daisies, a couple of white mini-calla lilies, and not to mention an occasional gather of mint to heighten her senses for the new week. On Monday's she would pass the flowers from the previous week onto her neighbors or plant them in their yard.

Today was Monday. Why was she consciously waiting for her "special delivery" while looking over at the past week's surprise: two pink dahlias. She felt like a house pet waiting on a treat.

"I need to get on with my day," she said to herself.

Elyse signed on to her computer and waited for the desktop to appear. As an urban development planner, her whole week could change with one email; and, with her life in a whirlwind, she felt like that change was going to show up in her inbox this morning. She plugged her MP3 player into the USB port and chose some music to assist the process—India Arie, Donald Lawrence, Goapele, Fred Hammond, and a few more. After making a quick-fix playlist, she entered her inbox.

"Let's see what's going on today," she said.

INBOX – New (18)

FROM:	William Macy
SENT:	Today 7:40 AM
MSG:	*Hey, Lys. Hope you had a great weekend. Let's meet up for lunch today to discuss the Brent project. 12:30?*

FROM:	Tayler Prentis
SENT:	Today 7:23 AM
MSG:	*I need the re-draft of your proposal ASAP. I'm working on the zoning codes, so don't worry about that part. Don't kill me, but the deadline has been moved up from Friday to this Wednesday. I know you can do it. You're the best in the business. Thanks!*
FROM:	Dad
SENT:	Yesterday 9:48 PM
MSG:	*Hey, Lysie. Just checking in.*
FROM:	Shara
SENT:	Saturday 8:30 PM
MSG:	*You won't believe what happened yesterday. Kaye caught us in the kitchen. She told me to stop hurting Daddy or she would call the police. *lol* I guess it's time for that talk. Lenn's sweating bullets about it already. When he tucked her in last night, he assured her that he wasn't*

> *hurt over and over again, but it took him a minute to get her back to sleep. Bless her heart. Anywho... hope you're having a good weekend, and don't forget about our date. Love you.*

FROM: William Macy
SENT: Friday 5:33 PM
MSG: *WHERE ARE YOU? I came by your office to run over the Brent project. Did you know they added a new apartment complex? Have a good weekend. I'm out.*

Elyse sighed as she scrolled through the remaining emails. Most of them consisted of the usual. "Do this," "Do that," and "I need this by..." She switched gears and checked her Internet mailbox. Clothing coupons sprinkled the page and she took the liberty of printing out one. "This might come in handy for Shara's party next month," she said to herself as she folded the printed coupon and placed it in her purse. As Elyse clicked away the junk mail from her inbox, the phone rang. She pressed the speakerphone button.

"Good Morning, this is Ms. Adams," she answered.

"Hey, Lysie."

"Hi, Daddy," Elyse replied with her child-like voice.

"How you doin' today, Honey?"

Right-click. Move to junk. Scroll down. Double-click. Skim. Delete.

"Fine. How are you?"

"I'm okay I guess," he stated. Elyse already knew what was coming next. She rolled her eyes and prepared for the clockwork conversation.

"What's wrong, Daddy?"

"My feet hurt and I can't find my shaving cream. You know I have to have my shaving cream."

"Have you looked in the refrigerator?"

"Now, Lysie, why would I look in there?" he asked in usual agitation.

"I don't know. I'm just thinking of where you could have put it down the last time you used it. Did you eat this morning?"

"I fixed some grits and eggs."

"Did you shave yesterday morning?"

"Yes."

"Go look in the refrigerator, Daddy."

"Lysie, I don't eat shaving cream! I'm not looking in that box!"

"Daddy, go look for me, okay? If I'm wrong, I'll take you out to lunch."

"You ain't got to beg. And you should want to take ya daddy out to lunch anyway. I'm all alone over here and don't nobody care about that. All ya'll wanna do is be on that Face Page Book 24-7. Folks live right down the street from each other and won't go see about them, but will send them an email. That's a shame and you know it."

Elyse heard his feet shuffle down the carpeted steps to the kitchen. He mumbled a little more along the way. She could picture the chilly air hitting his face and the shaving cream sitting in front of his eyes.

"You see it?"

"Yeah, I see it. How'd you know it was down there?"

"I don't know, Daddy. It was probably hot," she answered him.

She smiled on the other end of the phone. Ever since she was a little girl, her father had misplaced his shaving cream every other morning. He would grab it out of the bathroom and walk to her mother's bathroom to use the brighter lighting. On the way, he would often get sidetracked by Elyse or Shara getting ready for school or the morning news on television and put it down. When his daughters would find the shaving cream in the armoire or cabinet, it was okay, but the day they found it in the refrigerator, he claimed he placed it there on purpose to keep it cold. She and Shara would giggle at their father's forgetfulness, but let him keep his pride. Generally, his shaving cream could be found anywhere but in his bathroom.

"Don't make fun of your elders," he said semi-firmly.

"Yes sir," Elyse said, letting her smile seep through the receiver. He laughed at her efforts.

"So when are you coming down here?" asked her father.

She hated this part of the conversation. Ever since her mom died, her father's boldness of alerting the kids of his loneliness increased dramatically. It wasn't that the drive to Louisiana was too much to bear, but his whining was too much for her at times. When she did visit, he was never shy in mentioning that it took her "long enough" to get to him. She recalled one afternoon where he went too far according to her terms:

"By the time you come to visit, I could be dead and buried good in the ground."

"That's not fair, Daddy. You know I love you and I care about you very much. When you say things like that, it makes me not want to come down here."

"Well, it seems like that's what it takes to see my children nowadays. And I don't know what's wrong with Shara.

I can't tell you the last time she brought that grandbaby down here to see me. Kaye probably got children of her own by now," he said in frustration.

"Whatever you have to say to Shara, you say it her. I'm not in that," Elyse dismissed. "All I'm asking is that when I come to see you that we will make that time together as pleasant as possible. Can we do that, please?"

Elyse picked up her pen and began playing with the top, returning to the conversation at hand and answering his question.

"I was thinking that we would go out this weekend."

"Who?" he asked in amazement.

"Us!"

"Me and you?"

Elyse could tell he was truly surprised.

"Yes, Daddy, you and me."

"What we gon' do?"

"I thought I would take you fishing," she lied.

"Fishin'? We goin' fishin?" her father asked like an excited cub scout.

"No, I'm just playing. I did want to take you out to the lake and eat lunch though."

"You don't play around with a man and fishin'. What you got goin' sounds alright. What time I need to be ready?"

Mr. Adams and his daughter finalized their plans and departed in laughter and good spirits. Elyse turned to her computer and placed the date on her calendar. The beep on her phone confirmed that the calendars were in sync.

"Ms. Adams?"

Elyse turned around to find Trey, her assistant, with a disturbed look on his face.

"What is it, Trey?"

"It's Mr. Macy. He needs to see you immediately."

Elyse locked her computer screen and rushed her black pumps toward William's office.

***

Elyse arrived at William's office and closed the door behind her. He looked up from his desk with tears in his eyes. Her heart dropped. She only saw William's tears three times in his life: when everyone in his kindergarten class took things from his cubby box as a practical joke, when his friend was killed overseas while serving in the military, and when his mother died. She sat down in the chair in front of his desk and placed her hands upon his. They were cold and clammy.

"William."

He looked up at her as if the sound of his name was foreign. Elyse decided not to pressure him, but she figured his ordeal had something to do with his wife. She gently rubbed his hands in hopes of bringing some words to the surface. Her inability to be sensitive and nurturing tended to show up at the worst times. She was good at negotiating and debating, not hand holding. At the office, she was known as the "dog catcher" because she could bring any liar to the truth. She was unapologetic and brash, but still aesthetically pleasing enough to get catcalls from the construction workers next door. Sometimes she wished she had acquired the softy trait from her mother, but she figured she wouldn't be the tenacious businesswoman people had grown to respect if she had. Nevertheless, in times like these, that missing trait would come in handy. William looked at his friend's helpless face and attempted to gather the words to explain the urgent request of her presence.

"I think Rachel is cheating on me."

"What makes you think that? Do you have any proof?"

"Not yet."

"You already know what I'm going to say. No proof, no case."

"Lys, I know my wife. Something isn't right."

"William, I know *you*. You always construct a premature verdict and try to prove it later. This is one situation where you can't afford to do that."

"This is not one of those times. She's seeing somebody else and I'm going to get my proof."

William had always been the quiet type, but once he was determined about something, there was no stopping him. She sat back in her chair. As she released her spirit from the tension in the room, she prayed that William would find the answer he needed without anyone getting hurt.

CHAPTER 4

Their evening was sensual and exciting. After eating great food at the sports bar, the simple date turned into a good mix of sweet and salty banter between the two of them. Being the woman she was, Elyse was dead-set against Malcolm spending the night. She had actually extended her boundaries by riding with him on their date. Meeting up was always her preference.

"So I finally get to see where you lay your head," Malcolm said as they approached her home.

"And me without my blindfold. Where did I put that anesthesia?" Elyse patted the front and back pockets of her hip-hugging jeans.

Malcolm loved her sense of humor and enjoyed flirting with her wit. He wanted to see what else she could come up with on the fly.

"I hid it after I found the last victim behind the hedges."

Elyse snapped her fingers. "Man, I'm slipping," she replied with a straight face.

"You really should be a *little* more inconspicuous when you want to invite me inside."

Elyse laughed. "You've got some nerve. You should know by now that my middle name is 'Frank' and I don't have a problem telling you what I want."

"Is that so?" he said with a surprised look on his face.

"Can you recall a time where I've been evasive?"

Malcolm looked up into the night sky as if the stars would twinkle the answer to her question. He very much wanted to think of a moment where she hadn't been candid, just to counteract her perfect record. It wasn't working, and from the looks of it, the odds were not going to be in his favor for a while.

"Can you?" she asked rhetorically. "That's what I thought."

"Okay, you win. I can't think of a time where you haven't been straight up with me." He paused to give his thoughts a chance to form a sentence. "That's one of the things I like about you. You don't play games. I've never been with a woman like you, Elyse." His eyes drifted to the nearby flowerbed in her yard and he thought about the flowers in his mother's windowsill. Malcolm lifted his head and refocused. To his surprise, Elyse was fidgeting with her keys like a schoolgirl. "It's refreshing," he said, hoping his voice wouldn't squeak.

She looked up to acknowledge the honesty she heard. Her eyes connected with his and she felt vulnerability creep from under the blanket of his charisma. He was a bit out of his comfort zone. She couldn't quite put her finger on it, but he was experiencing something different. There was definitely a shift taking place within him.

"Thank you," she replied, not knowing what else to say. "I hope the refreshment continues." Another pause gently blew around them, carefully whispering between the optical journeys into each other's core. It was a soft exchange of spiritual uncovering. Now Elyse became the uncomfortable party between the two; nevertheless, she didn't break the visual cord connecting them.

"I hope so," Malcolm responded. "I like where this is going."

She blinked. The cord snapped. "Tonight, the only place *this* is going..." said Elyse, wanting to say 'me too,' but choosing an alternative, "...is to bed, alone."

"Hmm...I should have seen that coming."

"Thank you for a very nice day. I enjoyed myself. And you," she said smiling slightly.

He was happy to hear those words, yet maintained his cool temperature. "I enjoyed you too and I appreciate your time." The awkward pause after his words was thick as molasses.

"Have a good night and be safe until I see you again." Like a sweet benediction, he gazed into her eyes with care before modifying his stance to walk away. He was trying hard not to let too much of him show at once, but he couldn't help it. Malcolm was becoming an open field for her to find rest, and there was little he could do to stop it. And from what he could tell, she was beginning to feel the same toward him.

She opened her door with her key and entered the great room. Then she yielded to the urge and watched her date from the peephole. She peered out just in time to see him walking to his car parked at the peak of the arc driveway. He stepped into his vehicle with confidence and enchantment. He had dropped his guard and she seemed to have taken it well.

Before driving away, Malcolm glanced at her front door. Unbeknownst to him, Elyse's smile radiated and echoed the tingle in her heart just centimeters away from the door's peephole. "I really like him," she thought, "I just need to be careful. I want to be careful. I can't mess this up." She watched the red tail lights disappear down the neighborhood's winding streets and prayed that he thought of her with each mile he drove.

Elyse slowly removed herself from the door and walked towards the couch. She laid her keys in the small African bowl on the end table and made her way upstairs to the bedroom. An imaginary finger of guilt tapped her shoulder to remind her that the divorce had not been finalized and that she was retreating for the evening to the bed that was once shared. She had removed the pictures from the nightstands, but still had the jewelry box Kin had given her on their third wedding anniversary. She loved it too much to discard it, even though it had sentimental value. It was a heart-shaped box made of rich dark wood. The words *"loving is living"* were carved on its top, lining the bottom edges of the heart. She made a mental note of their love each time she passed it. She was used to looking in "the sandbox" soon after, like clockwork. "The sandbox" was a mixture of sand from all of the beaches they had visited together, beginning with their honeymoon and ending with their most recent trip to the coastline of Cocoa Beach, FL. There were six other seashores represented in "the sandbox"—St. Lucia, Jamaica, Key West, Savannah, Myrtle Beach, and Cape Cod. She and Kin had intimate moments at each destination. She was heartbroken when they stopped going because he suddenly "wasn't up for it."

A part of her wanted to enjoy the new love interest who had blown her way, but the house still smelled of Kin's last visit, and she could hardly forget the last time they were together.

***

The clouds looked like puffs of spun sugar sporadically yet strategically placed in the baby blue sky. Some resembled animals while others made Elyse think of attributes of Greek gods.

"That one looks like Achilles' heel," said Shara, pointing to the cloud in front of her. "Don't you think so?"

"Eh. A little. I was thinking Mercury's shoe. See the wings?"

"I guess I can see that," succumbing to Elyse's point of view, Shara continued her thought pattern. "So have you talked to Malcolm lately?"

"About a week ago. Why?" she answered, suspecting an underlying curiosity.

"Just asking. I just think he's a great guy, that's all. He's respectful, thoughtful, and open, not to mention he's beyond easy on the eyes."

Open. That word resonated in Elyse's mind and led to a threshold of emotional experiences. Taking note of this, Shara continued.

"Yes, open. He's good for you. You should take him seriously." She turned and faced her passenger window as if she had made a large deposit in her sister's cerebral account and was waiting for it to clear.

"Shara, if I didn't know any better, I would think that you were rushing me! I'll take him as I please right now. I don't want things to go too fast, ya know?"

"You've already slept with the man! What more is there to rush into?"

"You know it's deeper than that. Sure, it started off as a one-night thing, but I think I want more than that. And the scary thing is I believe he could give it to me. I just feel like I'm putting the cart in front of the horse, like I'm taking a morning-after pill and hoping for the best. I slept with him before I got a chance to know him. But what's crazy is he's doing the exact opposite of what I was expecting. He wants to talk and go out, you know, see more of me. He actually called, asked me out again, and wanted more than another 'sex meeting.' That's just something I didn't expect. Then there's Kin. The divorce isn't final and I'm thinking about another man. The sad part is I don't even feel bad about it. What kind of Christian am I, Shara?"

Her sister slightly tilted her head back to marinate, and then picked her words carefully like fresh flowers plucked from the side of a winding path and placed in a bouquet.

"I understand the whole Christian thing. It's different and I believe in my heart that you also find it refreshing. There's nothing wrong with taking your time. Unfortunately, you're brushing him off. Malcolm has extended his hand and mind to you and his heart is soon to follow. According to what you've told me, he's never asked you for commitment, just opportunity. All I'm asking is for you to consider opening the door to that opportunity he is presenting before you. No pressure or hassle about the future. It's way too soon to tell all of that. But I believe the opportunity will be worth any time and energy you can give at this point, large or small."

Elyse let Shara's words simmer. She didn't respond verbally. Her silence was the confirmation her sister was looking for. With that conversation at peace, Shara changed the subject matter.

"Thanks for the shopping. Lunch was perfect and I couldn't have asked for a prettier day."

"Me neither. And you're welcome. You know I love our dates. You always stretch me a little more than I expect and my cheeks end up being sore from laughing. Happy birthday, baby girl!" she replied smiling towards her before looking back at the road.

"I love you too, Honey," said Shara, as they pulled up to her home front. "I'll talk to you later on this week. I can't wait to hear about your date with Mr. Harrison tonight."

Elyse laughed at her sister's prediction. "We'll see."

"I know we will, because you're going to call me with the news that you had a wonderful time, and how he blew your mind among other things."

Elyse shook her head in embarrassment. "Get out of my car."

Shara gave her sister a nasty face and a kiss on the cheek. "You just make sure you're at my party next week and not somewhere with your nose wide open."

"Good*bye*, Shara," she replied, flicking the switch to the power windows. Her sister pointed her finger at her and it caught Elyse's attention before driving away. Deep down, Elyse could only hope that Malcolm would blow her mind plus anything else he wanted.

***

Shara walked into the house to find Lenn looking at a pornographic video on the computer. She rolled her eyes to his mechanical action. Ever since he lost his job, Lenn had increased his porn exposure in clear sight by two days a week and didn't bother to hide his magazines and movies anymore. At first, she looked over his indulgences as a way to release tension and she figured he wasn't harming anyone as long as he shielded Kaye from his antics. Some of the images on the screen were explicit, but at this point of their marriage, she was no longer disturbed by them.

"I thought you were aggravated with us womenfolk," Shara sarcastically reminded him of his previous words.

"Well, these women don't talk."

Shara looked at him with a serious "oh, really" response. She was appalled that he would come back with an implication of her talking too much. His fingertips lightly tapped at the mouse, clicking through pictures of nude women in various sexual positions. She was repulsed at the sight of his mindless enjoyment, as if a minor sector of his brain was being fondled and her husband was not in his body.

"I'll keep that in mind the next time you want to *talk* in bed," Shara retorted. She walked out of the living room with a monkey on her back, and the monkey was telling her that her husband was travelling down a spiral staircase of cancerous evil. Some *thing* had tapped into his psyche. She got the feeling that the "thing" was meticulously and relentlessly severing nerves and short-circuiting the husband she married ten years ago. His judgment and cognition were being re-wired and she carried that monkey of truth to their bed alone.

CHAPTER 5

The sunlight spread its rays like fingertips and waved slowly in front of her closed eyes, beckoning for Elyse's morning participation. She slowly stepped out of her REM sleep and into mild consciousness. Her body still felt heavy since she had just slept like a brick. Then a lukewarm pair of lips kissed her softly on the nape of her neck. She remembered a dream that began like this once before, so she decided to revel in it. Until the voice appeared.

"Good Morning."

It was a deep, smooth, breathy, masculine voice that transposed a common morning greeting into a warm and erotic salutation. So she decided to reply to the dream with a "Good Morning" herself.

The lips kissed her neck again in satisfaction of her response and she lightly moaned as she exhaled, gently smiling. He placed his right hand on her right shoulder and began to caress her body *au naturel* beneath the cloud-like covers.

Her nerve endings awakened and were petitioning her body to writhe in enjoyment, but she refrained from doing so. After all, it was just a dream. She absolutely enjoyed his hands on her canvas. The lips kissed her right shoulder and then walked their way up to the area behind her ears, just below her lobe. She smiled again in agreement. Feeling the skin on her cheeks, she reached back and lightly tapped the tip of his nose in affirmation. He continued his affectionate effect on her. This definitely wasn't a dream. In between his sweet tongue brushes and his lips lightly skimming her ear, Malcolm whispered, "It's 6:34. How do you feel?"

"Like I don't want to go into the office this morning," she answered. "Thanks for the wakeup call. I could use fifteen more minutes."

"You're welcome. I'm going to take a shower. I'll wake you up at 6:50. Take your time."

"Thank you so much."

"No problem," he replied, sealing his response with another kiss on her shoulder.

The voice and the lips and the warmth that connected them retracted slowly away from her body and out of the bed. Immediately, the echo of his soul was missed. She slipped into a light sleep, psyching herself out that the previous evening's sexual encounter did indeed happen. And she was still on the scene. Her eyes flung open. Out of the window, she could see the green trees surrounding his home. She barely knew him, but was comfortable enough to lie in his bed for an extra fifteen minutes as he prepared for the day. That was definitely not the norm. Elyse rose from the bed to find that she did not have to put out an A.P.B. for her unmentionables, but that they were laid neatly in the open nightstand drawer next to the bed, and her formal gown was hung on the back of the door. They had attended a charity auction the night before and decided to continue their evening at his home. She would be lying to herself if she said it wasn't an enjoyable and pleasurable experience. Unexpected, again, but definitely not regretted. Then the guilt set in louder than the water spraying from his showerhead. "And you call yourself a Christian," it said to her. She looked upward, naked and embarrassed, and said to the heavens in a deep exhale, "God, I'm so sorry." The words barely trickled from her lips and into the air above her head. "I sure hope He heard me," she thought. "I know He saw everything." With that horrible truth, Elyse covered her head with the top layer of the love-soaked bed linen.

***

Elyse looked at her watch and sighed. "Six-thirty already. I've got to get out of here," she said to herself. She organized three small stacks of papers, put them in a folder labeled "PRIORITY," and put the folder on the left side of her desk. She then reached across her desk and changed her inspirational flip calendar to the next date. It read:

Maintain your gate of peace.

"Hmm...perfect for tomorrow's busy-ness," she thought. Then, the phone rang.

"Hello?" she answered.

"Hey you! Happy Birthday!"

She sighed. "Hello, Kin and thank you." She then asked, completely out of courtesy, "How are you doing today?"

"I'm doing well, thanks. How about you?"

"Fine."

"That's a good thing. So what are your plans, Birthday Girl?"

"Why do you ask?" she replied quickly.

"Lys, I've known you for eleven years. I always ask you that question."

"I didn't think the question would continue after we parted ways."

"Some things will never change, like your happy birthday wishes from me. If you prefer otherwise, by all means, just tell me," he requested.

She sighed again, only this time it was a little heavier. "Kin, I'm adjusting. That's all I'm saying."

A seriously awkward pause put its hands between their phone lines.

"So am I. Elyse, I just called to say happy birthday. I'm sorry for interrupting your *adjustment*."

"You don't have to respond that way. I appreciate your thought and your call," she managed to say. "Your birthday wishes are always welcomed. Thank you, Kin."

A little bruised from her initial coldness, Kin replied, "You're welcome. Enjoy your day and take care."

"You too." With that, she firmly hung up the phone's receiver and stared at it. After two minutes passed, she placed her hand on the phone and patted it twice. She wanted to call him back, but couldn't rationalize a reason to do so. She retrieved her purse from the base drawer of her desk and got her keys from the top drawer. She double-checked her office security card on the right side of her suit pants. Elyse lightly moaned in an attempt to expel remnants of the phone conversation as she rose from her chair and made her way to the elevator. She remembered tomorrow morning's meeting and pressed the elevator button with a little more fervor.

***

"William, you okay? I noticed your car was still here when I left the office yesterday."

William's face was boyish. He had no facial hair and his curly auburn hair was tousled. He was typing furiously at the computer and his eyes were zeroed in beyond the screen. Elyse walked around his desk, disregarding the fact that he was her superior. She noticed Rachel's email address at the top. William, intensely engaged in the moment, had yet to acknowledge her presence. Afraid that she would stop his purge, she decided to walk back around to the front of his desk and have a seat. The last thing she wanted to do was come between an angry friend and his thoughts. Ten minutes went by and she began to tap her fingers on his desk. Like a determined drone, he continued his email. Finally, Elyse got up and walked toward the door. She had other things to do and decided to come back later.

"Don't leave."

Elyse paused at the door like a cat with heightened senses. William's voice was raspy and sharp. She could tell that he had either been screaming or had just spoken for the first time that day. She retracted her hand from the doorknob and turned around.

"I can come back later if you need to finish."

"I'm good," he replied dryly and still typing.

"Oh-kaaayyyyyy," Elyse said slowly as she slinked back towards the chair and sat down, this time with her legs crossed. She was never the most patient individual. That trait belonged to her sister. She loved William and hated to see him in obvious distress, but she had a lunch date with Malcolm and wanted to wrap up a few things before heading out. A quick look at the clock—eight minutes to spare. She figured she would take a chance and begin the conversation. "So, what's wrong? What did Rachel do now?"

"It's not what she did. It's what I did. I kicked her out."

"You did what?!"

"I found her in the house with another man. Now she's sending me these stupid emails." He sounded so mechanical and dry that it scared her. She didn't want to pry open the door of their marital unrest, but she just had to know what happened. Elyse knew her friend like the back of her hand, so if he kicked her out, it wasn't just because she had cheated on him. The deed had been compounded with other actions. She looked at her watch and gauged that she had exactly seven minutes to formulate an image of the matter.

"I know what you're about to do. I don't want to talk about it."

"Then why did you ask me not to leave?!"

"I wanted you to read this email before I send it," William replied, fingers typing.

Elyse sighed with annoyance and walked to the computer screen. Knowing her seven-minute grace period was almost up, she figured the email would get a quick scan at best. Skimming the first paragraph evolved into reading the message in its entirety. She was amazed at how cool William was when he asked, "So, is it ready?" He blinked like a programmed android. She couldn't stop looking at the words on the screen.

"HELLO! Is it ready to send?!" he blurted, tapping his fingers on the desk. Elyse's phone rang. Malcolm's number was just the "out" she needed. She patted William on the back and proceeded toward the door.

"If you're prepared for the response, then you're ready to send it. I'll be back in an hour."

***

Asian paper lanterns hung from the ceiling of the Petersons' home. *Kindred the Family Soul* played in the background and everyone was enjoying the surroundings. Laughter and the sound of glasses clinking filled the air. Dancing was inevitable. The couple of the hour looked separately happy.

"Sis, great party!" Elyse complimented.

"Thanks! Lenn kept saying he didn't want to have a party, but I just couldn't let our tenth wedding anniversary go by without doing something," replied Shara.

"Yeah, ten years is a big deal. And you're right, it should be celebrated. Cute lanterns. Where did you get them?"

"Remember when I went to California last year? They were having an Asian bazaar and I picked them up on our way to the airport. There were some really good vendors there."

"That's right," Elyse recalled. "That's when you got me that kimono."

Shara nodded in agreement. She lightly placed her hand on Elyse's back. "I'm going to float around a bit. Have some more wine and relax," Shara ushered.

Elyse was trying her best not to feel out of place. The living room was filled with couples. She decided to sit down on the bay window seat to keep from drawing attention to herself. Shara floated around the room as promised, like the social butterfly she was, making sure everyone was having a good time. She refilled a few drinks and inserted laughter in just the right conversations. She had always been the extrovert of the family. She got that attribute from their father; but ever since their mother died from breast cancer, he didn't seem to exhibit that part of his personality anymore.

"Girl, *what* are you over here pondering?" Shara intercepted.

"Nothing," Elyse smiled to give Shara reassurance.

"Hm. Doesn't seem like it to me. But that's cool. We'll talk later. In the meantime, I need your help with something in the kitchen."

Shara leaned over and whispered the update in Elyse's ear. Lenn had been sneaking upstairs to watch porn all day.

Elyse's mind burned with disturbing images of her sister's husband.

"I *don't* want to know about this."

"I'm not asking you to get in the middle of it. I'm just asking you to help me keep an eye on him. You know, if you see him moving away from the party, strike up a conversation or something." Elyse could see the masked concern on her sister's face.

"This is between you and Lenn. We never had this conversation."

Shara leaned back against the kitchen counter in disbelief. She rolled her eyes and crossed her arms.

"I never thought I would see the day where we couldn't talk about anything under the sun."

"We can," Elyse whispered loudly. "I just don't want to get involved!" The noise of the party seemed to get louder as their emotions progressed.

"I don't want you to get 'involved.' I need your help! This is serious!"

"I know, but Shara, this is some heavy stuff!"

"Fine." With that word, she was left to stew in her thoughts alone. Shara's long, colorful skirt flowed as she walked with ease through the hallway and disappeared into the crowd.

Elyse sipped on her homemade margarita with her ankles crossed. When the doorbell rang, she found it to be the perfect opportunity to make amends with her sister by answering the door on her behalf. She grabbed one of the party bags lying on the kitchen island, plastered a smile on her face, and headed toward the front of the house. Her poise dropped when she opened the door, so Shara stepped in behind her.

"Hi! Welcome! Let me take your coat." Shara smiled, extended her hand in hospitality, and led the couple past the guests in the front room. "What would you like to drink? We have margaritas, martinis, and daiquiris on the menu. You two can get in the game while I fix your drinks."

"Let me help you, Sis," Elyse managed to mutter. She followed her towards the kitchen.

"What are you doing?!" shouted Elyse in a harsh whisper.

"I'm fixing drinks," Shara replied, pouring Vodka.

Elyse stepped back and placed her hand on a vacant space on the kitchen island.

"I invited him before the divorce! God knows I didn't think he would still show up!"

"How could you do that, Shara?!" She walked away from the kitchen island. Shara was a genuine soul, but sometimes Elyse wanted nothing more than to smack her older sister back into her mother's womb so she could start over in developing common sense.

"You better get rid of him or I'm leaving," Elyse imposed.

"What do you mean 'get rid of him'? He's not a dog, Lys. I can't just *uninvite* the man."

"The hell you can!" Elyse said loudly.

"Girl, keep it down! Look, I'm sure he'll leave soon. His date looks like she's under age anyway."

"Now you listen to me," she squared her sister in the eyes and used her finger for reiteration. "I don't want to see him, do you understand? I don't want to see him, smell him, touch him, nothing. Do you understand me?"

Shara calmly finished preparing the drinks. She placed her hand on the kitchen counter and spoke sincerely to her sister's anxiety.

"The man is here with a guest. You're going to have to grow up about this. You can't dart in and out of shadows forever. It's been three months since he moved out. Be in control of YOU and get it together! Put your big girl panties on and let's go out there and have a good time. Okay? It's *my* party, not his."

Elyse knew her sister was right, but didn't want to admit it. Knowing her sister's stubbornness, Shara initiated the hug her sister needed. Elyse let out a big sigh and hugged her back with what little trust she could muster.

"Let's get this over with," said Elyse, "and you owe me a pedicure."

Shara proceeded to walk out of the kitchen with the drink orders. Before leaving the threshold, she gave her sister a quick flash of a smile.

"Make that a full spa treatment," Elyse muttered under her breath.

CHAPTER 6

"Good Morning in here!" Malcolm walked into the front door of his mother's house and was instantly greeted with her loving warmth, as always.

"Mornin', Baby! How you doin' today?" Mrs. Daniels came out of the kitchen wiping her hands on a dish towel.

"Doing fine, Mama," he answered and kissed her cheek. "What about you? How's your wrist?"

"Awww, I'll be alright, Malcolm. When you get this old, you just shake off the small stuff."

"Mama, burning your wrist isn't small stuff. Let me see it." He held out his hand, ushering her to honor his command. She projected her right arm out for him to examine. In her mind, she was rolling her eyes at his oversensitivity. In contrast, the gratefulness of having a caring son overrode her instinct to brush him off, and she created a pleasant expression on her face.

"So whatcha think, Doc. Am I gon' live?" she said facetiously.

"That's not funny, Mama. The skin is healing nicely. Just be careful carrying those pots from the stove, especially when they haven't cooled. I'm just glad it wasn't worse."

"God has been taking care of me longer than you've been alive, Son. And he ain't stoppin' no time soon. So you just rest your head," she said, reaching out with her injured hand to touch the top of his head. Knowing her 5'4" frame couldn't access his 5'10" stature, he bent down slightly to grant her action. "So tell me about yourself." With that, she turned around and walked toward the den. "How the new job treatin' ya?"

"Job's treating me fine. Just work as usual. Nothing much going on around there except my time and energy."

"Well, that's good. You just keep on. God's still watching, so you keep doing," she replied, handing him a dose of encouragement. "We still on for that cruise?"

"We sure are, Pretty Lady."

She beamed at the thought of cruising the Mediterranean. She had an adventurous spirit and enjoyed experiencing new things. She had always loved to travel. "I sure am lookin' forward to it. I bought some shorts the other day and packed them in the suitcase."

"Shorts?! You packed shorts already?"

"Yeah, Malcolm. I packed shorts! What's so hard to believe about that?"

"Well first of all, you must think you grown for real if you're buying shorts. Showing *leg* is prohibited on this trip, Mrs. Daniels. You can't show your knees on this trip. Then, on top of that, you're packing and the trip is six months away. You must be really ready for this vacation!"

"Aww, Malcolm, hush," she chuckled at his antics and shooed him with her hands. "I'm good and grown, honey. *And* I'm gon' wear some shorts on this cruise! You ain't ready for me!"

"I must not be," Malcolm replied. "You're obviously going to be a handful. Maybe I should start packing tonight."

"Maybe you should if you want to keep up with me. I plan on having the time of my life." Mrs. Daniels raised her arms up, snapped her fingers and closed her eyes, then swayed to the foreseen party music on the ship.

"You're a mess, Mama."

"I know, Shuga. And you love it, too," she responded, still snapping her fingers. "Maybe when we get back, you can get to work on getting me some grandchildren. You seeing anybody?"

"Not really. I'm seeing this one woman, but it's nothing serious right now. We're just enjoying time spent with one another."

"What's her name?"

"Here we go," Malcolm prepped himself as he sat on the couch. "Elyse."

"Elyse what?"

"Elyse Adams?"

"That's pretty. Who her folks?"

"Mama, you don't know her folks."

"How you know who I know?"

"You probably don't know her folks."

"You don't know *what* I know! Who her folks?"

"I don't know. I just know her. She has a sister named Shara."

"Is she married?"

"No, ma'am."

"She have any children?"

"No."

"She tall?"

"She's a few inches taller than you."

"Hmm. She got good skin?"

"Mama."

"I'm just askin'. Ain't nothing wrong with askin' questions. You need a woman who can take care of herself. If she takes care of herself, she'll take good care of you too. And you know I want some tall grandsons…"

"Mama."

"Alright, alright. So does she have a good job?"

"She does live well."

"What does she do?"

"She's an urban development planner. She is part of a team of people who are responsible for city revitalization projects, turning old buildings and barren lots into something useful and profitable for the community."

"Hmmm. That sounds nice," Mrs. Daniels nodded with approval. "She must work hard like you, Son."

Lightly laughing to himself, he replied sweetly. "She does, Mama."

"Well that's what you need."

Malcolm placed his hands on his knees underneath the table, preparing to stand.

"So when am I going to meet this young lady?" Mrs. Daniels interrupted.

"You know the rule. You can meet anyone I'm dating whenever you want. You always have and always will have first knowledge. Just know it's not serious. I like her, don't get me wrong. We're cool right now."

"I understand. How about you invite her over here after church for Sunday dinner."

"I don't know if we're quite on that level yet. Let's invite her to church a little later on."

"What's wrong with inviting her to church?"

"Nothing's wrong with it, Mama. I'm just saying we're not there yet."

"You got to be on a particular level to go to church with somebody now?"

"No, ma'am. I just don't want anyone to be walking me down the aisle so soon. You know people talk at church. As soon as you bring someone of the opposite sex, they stare at you and the person until you sit down, then they want to put you in wedding attire before the offering."

"Malcolm, you can't worry about them folks out there at the church. They're going to say whatever they want to say whenever they want to say it. It don't matter what they say if you know who you are. You bring her on to church and make her and *yourself* comfortable."

"I'll let you know when we're coming. How about that?"

Taking his hint, Mrs. Daniels smiled and walked into the kitchen to check on the cornbread she put in the oven upon Malcolm's arrival. She lovingly cupped her son's chin on her way under the den's threshold.

"You need some help?" he asked.

"No, I'm alright, Baby. Just checkin' on this cornbread." The sound of the oven creaking open gave way to the warm and buttery smell of homemade cornbread with a touch of honey. The scent wrapped around his nose like an expensive silk handkerchief.

"Where's Mr. Daniels today?" Malcolm inquired.

"He's gone to get a haircut. He should be back in about an hour or so."

"That's alright. I'll catch him next time. Gimme some sugar, Pretty Lady." Malcolm walked into the kitchen. She extended her cheek to him and received the bittersweet denouement of his visit.

"I love you, Son."

"I love you too, Mama. Call you tomorrow."

CHAPTER 7

"Do you see this?!" Shara held up the back of her left hand, fingertips up, showing the wedded stone like a hypnotist. Lenn stood there unresponsive, blank-faced, and drunk.

"DO YOU SEE THIS?!" Shara screamed. She grabbed the wrist of his married hand and pressed it against the palm of her left. The wedding set clinked with force like two iron swords in battle. "You see this right here? We're in this together. You don't do things like this without me knowing, Lenn! I am with *you*. I am welded to *you*. I complement *you*. And you can't go running around with half of yourself making whole, domino-effect decisions." She left his hand up there, letting his wrist go in disgust. With that punctuation, she turned and walked away from him. Lenn's pornographic addiction totaled $949.00; $755 of it was spent on phone calls alone, the rest in movies. Shara, still livid, walked lightly and slowly from the fireplace, into the hallway that led to their kitchen.

"So now I have to figure out how we're going to replace $950. Or do you have plans for our savings account, too?"

"What are trying to say, Shara? I'm not capable of bringing in money for the house? That's just like something you would say. You *would* throw that up in my face."

She turned to look at him across the room and began to walk toward his ignorance.

"I'm not saying that you can't find the money, and I'm not saying that you can't *work* for the money. What I *am* saying is that you spent money that was set aside for Kaye's fund! That's the problem." She squared up in front of him and continued. "That is a MAJOR problem. I can handle your sporadic online lust-capades and late night crawl-ins from the movies, but this? You know the rule and you know the budget. What's so hard about sticking to that?! And another thing I'm saying is that you didn't even have a plan of replacing it! You just spent it as if I wasn't going to notice that $950 would be missing from the account! I have a problem with that! You broke the rule! We had an agreement, Lenn. I handle the bills, you handle yourself. Now you go and screw that up too! Furthermore, you have a deeper problem if you don't see it the same way!"

Shara removed herself from his presence with one last notion. Almost in a whisper, she said "I need your head to be clear. Fast. Or I will figure out a way to replace *you*, and you won't have to worry about having this conversation again. Kaye and I can and will live without you if need be. You remember that the next time you look at those…*girls*." She dropped off bags of accumulated anger in front of her husband's mental porch and stormed toward the staircase. After reaching the top, she made the turn into Kaye's room. It had "Special Kaye" in big pink letters on the wall, along with pictures labeled "Mommy" and "Daddy."

She stood there and watched Kaye's face reflect brightly from the sunlit window and her computer monitor. She waved the checkered flag in her racing mind and focused on the daughter in front of her, their beautiful creation.

She noticed Kaye's face appearing distressed.

"Whatcha doin', Babe?"

Kaye turned around from the computer screen. "Playing *The Spelling Tree*. I'm stuck. I don't know this word."

"What happens when we get stuck?" Shara asked her.

"We think and we try," Kaye responded obediently.

"Very good. Smart Girl." Shara released a small smile of admiration. Her daughter had turned out to be such an intellectual, just like her father. So bright and so refreshing was her beautiful mind and loving heart. She just couldn't understand how Lenn, someone so brilliant, could do self-defeating things and be angry at others for the outcome. And here she was, his seed, being diligent enough with her own time to study spelling words before starting Kindergarten.

"Do you want me to help you?"

"Yes Ma'am. Thank you."

"You're welcome, Baby. But it's going to cost you."

"Cost? That's money. I only have a quarter," she said with a worried face.

Shara chuckled lightly. "Cost doesn't always mean money, Kaye," she replied. "But you're right. Cost means trading something you have for something you want."

"Oh. Okay. How much is *your* cost?"

"The big hug full of love. Mommy needs that right now."

Kaye's smiled beamed with assurance. "I can do that!"

"I thought you could! So where is it?"

"Right here!!!" Kaye leapt from her desk chair and ran into the open arms of her mother. She picked her up and held her close to her heart. Shara soaked her angry heart into that embrace while remnants of the previous conversation played in a low timber in her mind. She squeezed the sweet four-year-old innocence a little tighter to block out the noise. Kaye's little arms attempted the same intensity. She placed her hands over her mother's ears and whispered, "Guess what."

"What?" Shara whispered back.

"I love you this much," she said, holding her arm out and squeezing Shara's neck.

"Wow! That's a lot of love, little girl. You think we ought to share with Daddy?"

"Nahhhhhhhh! He got you! I'm passing down!"

"Ohhh, okay. That's how it works. I'll be sure to 'pass it down' when I see him."

***

"Today is a new day," Elyse said to herself when she woke up that morning. She scanned the bedroom and made up her mind that she needed to clear out a few things. Actually, a lot of things. Kin had left a couple of ties in the closet and the "daughter-in-love" gift from his mother still sat on her nightstand. It was a small flower pot with clovers sprouting in it. She had painted the couple's wedding date on the terra cotta exterior. When she had a stroke, she made it for Elyse during rehabilitation and instructed her to look upon it anytime she felt like giving up on her marriage.

"I know she made it for me, but it's got to go," she said fervently.

Elyse sat straight up in the bed and reached for the flower pot. She had a divine urge to throw it away. That's it. She was going to throw it away that instant. On her way to the bedroom door, she passed "the sandbox."

"You've got to go too," she noted. "I can visit new beaches. I could use some new sand anyway." She picked up "the sandbox" and walked downstairs toward the kitchen. On her way down the steps, she passed by a picture on the wall of her, Kin, and a group of mutual friends.

"Sorry. You too." She lifted it from its nail and continued her trek toward the kitchen trash can.

Elyse put the items on the kitchen island and retrieved a large trash bag.

"It's time to get rid of this stuff," she muttered with disgust and confidence.

She put the items in the bag and proceeded to round up anything that reminded her of her estranged husband. All of his remaining ball caps and unopened toiletries were gathered for charity. She figured he wouldn't miss the stuff his brother forgot to collect. After all, it had been months since he left her to pick up the pieces of her soul from that floor. Factor in two hours' worth of no-holds-barred purging and she was already feeling hungry. Elyse fixed herself a sandwich and grabbed her MP3 player. She needed a quick jog to kick in more endorphins for the next leg of her excavating adventure.

Before she left, she lit a soft pink candle in the great room. A cream-colored ribbon of silky wax wrapped around it and the smell of strawberries and cream frolicked from the flickering flame.

"Yeah. That's more like it," she thought as she closed the front door.

As she jogged around the neighborhood, she heard some catcalls from a passing car. Instinctively, she turned the volume up a notch and steadied her pace. Damien Marley was on rotation at the moment and she was determined to make the most of her workout.

***

Elyse returned to her steps to find Kin's car parked out front. She had forgotten to change the locks and alarm codes since his brother vowed to return for Kin's leftovers.

Her heart began to palpitate and her gut turned sour. She unlocked the door and walked inside, forcing her head to tilt upward in pseudo-fortitude.

"Hello in here!" she shouted. Her voice echoed around the great room like a ball in a racquetball court. Kin came downstairs with his ball caps stacked in hand.

"Were you going to throw these away?" he asked.

"No, I was going to give them to the foster care center down the street. Your brother didn't pick them up when he came for your things, so I put them aside as I was cleaning up." She explained.

"Oh," he said looking down at the hats, "Well, I just came by to get them. He called last night and said he forgot to get them."

"Oh, okay" she responded, breathy from fatigue. "If you see anything else you want, help yourself. I'm trying to clear things out this weekend."

Elyse walked toward the refrigerator for a snack. She bent over and checked the bins in search of the plums she purchased earlier that week.

"Kaye must have eaten some," she thought.

She reached further back and moved the Greek yogurt aside and discovered the two plums she had hidden for herself. She smiled at her ingenious idea to tuck away a couple in the event that Kaye got a bit "happy" with the fruit. She bit into it and a trickle of juice dropped down her chin. She wiped it away with the sleeve of her sweat jacket. All the while, Kin was entranced by her from a distance. He had started the process of recovering his books from the bookcase in the great room, but was caught up in Elyse's glow and ritualistic behavior. She always craved fruit and water after a workout. Dropping off the books onto the couch, he walked casually toward the kitchen. Elyse had gone to the other side of the room for a glass. He strolled behind her and lightly placed his hands around her waist.

"I smell workout," he said with a grin.

"Perhaps you're too close then," she responded.

"You know that after-glow excites me, Lys." He caressed her shoulders and smelled her hair. "Vanilla Creme."

"Yeah, you're *really* too close. I'm going into the great room," she said.

Before she could shift her footing, he gently placed his hands on the counter, closing her in. He grazed his nose across the top of her left ear and exhaled lightly. Shivers ran up her spine like racecars on a mission.

"I think it's time for you to go." Elyse said calmly.

But Kin knew her body. Her strands of muscle, the language of her ankles, and the tightening of her thighs. He remembered that she loved peaches and honey and that she hated roses. His olfactory senses caught the subtle breeze of her perfume underneath her dewy sports jacket. As he kissed the collar of her neck, his left hand began a journey of recollection. He had the map to every curve of her body. The warmth of his breath summoned the custom pheromones that had lay dormant within her for seven months. When they rose from the surface of her skin, each had a capital "K" attached as if they had been anticipating this very moment. She turned around and lifted her face on the vertical plane like a puppet yielding to its master. Then she opened. He kissed her fingertips and she replied with kisses of her own on his shoulder. She missed his muscular arms enveloping her past and present concerns. Each time she attempted to control her body, he pressed another button to punctuate his intensity. Her head tilted back as Kin's tongue made circles around the nape of her neck.

"I really need to go," she exhaled.

"You live here," he whispered between kisses.

His fingers walked down the zipper of her jacket and she felt her femininity become exposed like loose marbles on the floor.

Elyse could barely retort verbally with her body responding in the opposite direction. "You're right, um…one of us has to go. We can't do this," she managed to reply before turning around.

"Are you sure about that?" Kin asked, moving his kisses to her shoulders.

As if on cue, Elyse's bra strap tipped over as if surrendering to his advancement. It was just the alarm she needed to awake from the trance.

"I can't, Kin. I just can't. I can't do this back-and-forth thing with you."

Kin stopped as if someone pressed pause on his game. "You're still my wife," he stated calmly. "So what's the problem?"

Elyse turned around and looked into his eyes. "The problem is I am a wife that you don't want."

She walked around the kitchen island and headed toward the front door. Her athletic shoes hit the marble floor like elephants searching for water. She had to get him out of the house and she couldn't do it with weak knees and heavy breathing. Elyse's hand touched the cold doorknob and pulled it open, only to find Kin standing over her with his right hand on the door. He pressed it shut.

"You still love me."

"Kin, no I do not. I just want something I can't have with you."

"Which is?"

"Love."

"Love?!" Kin said with a shocking look.

"Yes, Kin. Love. You don't love me. Remember?" Elyse said slowly, "You said that and made it clear. I've accepted it, so we just can't keep doing this. I don't belong to you anymore."

Kin looked into her eyes, but drifted off into space. His look confused her. It was if his mind clicked to auto-pilot.

He grabbed her arms and slowly squeezed them. His grip became tighter and tighter.

"Kin, stop it. You're hurting me!" Elyse said firmly. It usually worked, but something was different this time.

He yanked the right sleeve of her sweat jacket down to her elbow and proceeded to kiss her forcefully on her neck.

"KIN!" shouted Elyse, "STOP!! WHAT ARE YOU DOING?!" She struggled for freedom, but his frame was too much for her to repel. He yanked her left sleeve downward and his mouth bore down harder on her flesh. Her white tank top ripped as he grabbed a fist full of her clothing. Elyse screamed for Kin to cease, but it was no use. He spun her around with one swift jerk of the hand. This was happening. Again. As he tugged at her sweatpants, the elastic snapped and the pedometer on her waist shattered to the floor. His teeth broke the gentle skin on her chest and she could feel the sting of fresh blood hitting the air. He breathed heavily like a dog in heat, but uttered no words. She slinked down to the Italian marble floor; drained of the energy she had left from cleaning and jogging. She could barely fight to escape his grip. Tears raced down her cheeks and dripped like leaky water faucets on the back of his custom-tailored shirt.

"Kin! Please! Please stop!" she sobbed.

In the distance, the strawberry candle melted into a silky pink puddle and the night seemed to last forever in slow motion. Like her fighting spirit, the candle's flame minimally flickered before it expired for the evening.

CHAPTER 8

Elyse tied the laces on her orange and blue running shoes. She hadn't run with a partner since last summer and her shoes seemed to be elated to be out of the closet. She had washed her orange wristbands the night before and placed a bottle of water and a banana aside for the trek. On her way out, she caught the sight of the pink candle above the fireplace.

"I really can't keep doing this to myself," she thought as she proceeded out of the door.

One of the selling points of the house was that it was less than a mile away from a park. She basked in the picturesque bike ride on many Sunday afternoons, however this one was special. The birds seemed to sing a custom arrangement for her along the way and the breeze felt like a blow of grace. It made her hair dance and her soul feel free. Part of her was sad to park her bicycle. She began her usual breathing exercises to steady her body in preparation. She locked the chain and found a quiet spot underneath a shady acorn tree to sit and wait. Malcolm admired her from a distance. She was calm and focused. Before leaving his car, he stuck two pieces of gum in his phone case.

Elyse stood and welcomed Malcolm to the area.

"You can't give directions," he said in close proximity.

"You got here, didn't you? Get to stretching."

"I was hoping we would do that together."

"Are you being fresh?" she asked.

"Just telling you what I thought. Obviously catching is not your strong point," he retorted.

"I got your catch right here in these running shoes."

Malcolm chuckled in disbelief. "Mark my words, Ms. Adams. You *will* fall victim to the dirt today."

With those words, Elyse smiled mischievously and took off running. He admired her form as her feet hit the earth, and then followed behind her. They ran close to 3 miles side by side before taking a water break. When they reached the fourth mile, they stood near the park's manmade lake in silence, taking in the sunset and the intensity of the run. Two trips around the lake totaled one mile and both were competitive enough to tackle it before they departed.

"Ready?" he asked.

"Yeah. Let's go." She assured.

They ran around the first time with determination. Perspiration ran down their bodies and their socks were drenched. The heated humidity in the air coerced Malcolm to rethink his mission.

"I think I'm going to call it right here," he said, decreasing his speed.

"Aw c'mon! I could go one more! You can't do it?" She lightly punched his shoulder as she matched his speed. She then sped up to where he was behind her a few inches.

"Don't play. My body's just telling me to take the edge off."

"Let me see what you got then," she trotted on.

He picked up minimal speed and began breathing out of his nose. They ran several feet before her body and mind decided that they had had enough. Her eyesight dimmed and her limp body fell to the ground.

***

He drew bathwater for her in his garden tub and lit two candles at the faucet's end. The drops of peppermint and eucalyptus oils created an invigorating yet soothing fragrance that filled the bathroom. He returned to the guest bedroom to retrieve Elyse. She had fallen asleep on the bed after the car ride to his place. She was tired and her fully-clothed body had shut down for her.

"Elyse," he whispered, sliding his hand down on her back. "Let me take you to the bathroom."

Muffled through her arms, which were propping her head, she replied sleepily, "I don't have to use the bathroom." Lying on her stomach, she turned her head away from him.

"There's a warm bath waiting to help you feel better."

She returned her face towards him and looked up in heavy-eyed surprise. "You have a bath waiting for me?"

"I just followed the bathtub's orders. The excitement was too much to bear, so it summoned me to retrieve you," he jabbed.

"Yeah, okay," she said, getting up slowly with the help of his arms. When she finally stood on her feet, a sincere "thank you" fell from her lips.

"No problem," he said with a nurturing glance. "Can you make it okay?"

She looked upon his face to ensure her gratitude was felt. Her head throbbed and she had bruises and scrapes that he had cleaned and bandaged.

"You're welcome to use anything. Hope you enjoy it."

When Elyse went into the guest bathroom, the fragrance from the oils awakened her mind. He had laid a mint green towel next to the chocolate facecloth on the right-wall shelves. Underneath them were variations of lotions and oils for her to choose from. The shelving was stained wood and they appeared to be floating. The walls were a sweet vanilla cream kissed with honeydew artwork hanging on them like inviting ripe fruit on a tree in season. The flooring was laid with slated stones like a landscaped path. The lighting was soft and pleasant. She had never seen a ceiling fan in a bathroom before, but it definitely was a nice addition to the tropically-inspired lavatory, especially with its coffee brown leaf-like blades. She looked to her left and blinked twice. The sink was a clear basin perched on top of the vanity, ornamented with a rustic brown goose-neck faucet gracefully gazing inside of it. A faux palm tree stood in the back corner near the toilet. Bamboo shoots were casually placed against the back wall next to the olive-colored chaise. On its right was a small refrigerator the size of an end table masked as a distressed wooden floor cabinet. The chaise was positioned in such a way that an admirer could enjoy his or her human work of art in the oval-shaped jetted tub further right. And yet, next to the tub was another refrigerator posing as a piece of furniture to merely set drinks upon. It was beautiful. She was amazed that she had the opportunity to enjoy her solitude in such surroundings. She had been to his bedroom, but not his master bath upon her preference.

Her mind and body slipped again into comfort and she drifted off to sleep in the garden tub. She awakened to a towel laid gently over her breasts, reaching down to her upper thighs.

He had covered her, but she didn't feel exposed after becoming so relaxed in the water. The steam and the oils took her to a place of serenity, a place that felt like home without the physical structure. Then the sounds of ethereal silence were interrupted abruptly by yet another beautiful sound.

"Elyse?"

It was Malcolm. He had been sitting at the edge of the tub for a while, it seemed. She immediately pressed the floating towels against her body.

"I wasn't comfortable with you falling asleep in here alone, so I hope you didn't mind. You're not drowning on my watch."

She smiled. "Thanks. Actually I'm ready to get out, so if you don't mind," she gestured with her tone and eyes for him to move towards the door.

Ignoring her communication, he unfolded and extended the mint green towel for her to come from the water. "I won't look at your body. I promise."

His eyes locked into hers and they beckoned her to follow his nonverbal request. She arose from the water like a baptized queen, poised and trusting of her servant. Malcolm maintained that trust until she safely stepped onto the mat; then, he transferred the towel to her hands, never once breaking their connection.

"I'll wait for you downstairs. Take your time." With that said, he left the room. Amazed that he refrained from repeating their previous sexual impulses, she dried and moisturized her frame, then slowly put on the t-shirt and sweatpants he had laid out for her. They were too large for her, but she was appreciative of the thought and his hospitable gesture. As she walked down the levitating staircase leading to the den, he laughed softly.

"My sister was here from Washington last week and left that outfit in the laundry room. It doesn't look so bad on you," he managed to say before laughing more. Embarrassed, but smiling, she confirmed his joke.

"I do wear it well, don't I?" she said, striking poses on the impromptu catwalk. He smiled, almost revealing his mind's transformation. "Yes, you do," he said, as he refocused on her needs and proceeded with his train of thought. "So how are you feeling?"

"I feel a lot better than I did on that pavement."

"I bet you do, Ms. 'I can go one more mile.'" He mocked.

"I could have gone another mile if it wasn't so hot outside. You were just afraid that I would outlast you," she replied.

"We both know that I can outlast you at more than just running."

Bashful and taken aback, Elyse retorted with a glance of fierceness.

"I do believe that's correct, at least according to my last recollection. Let's read the minutes." Malcolm pretended to flip vertical pages in a court reporter's book. "'Malcolm, just…just wait a minute. I've, I've got to catch my breath.'" He mimicked her voice and mannerisms so well that she couldn't be offended.

Even more embarrassed, she replied, "I thought you said we weren't going to relive those moments."

"I did. But that doesn't mean I've forgotten them."

Silence crept and sat between them. They both looked at it, awkwardly. Elyse interrupted it by clearing her throat.

"I'm sorry. I am trying here," he admitted.

"It's not just you. I'm doing my best over here as well," Elyse said, looking down.

"The power of God, and only the power of God, is truly keeping me right now," sighed Malcolm. "It's definitely not me. But I want to do this right. I made a promise that I would love you, Elyse, beyond the physical. So bear with me. And my memories."

She wanted to wrap her arms around him and enjoy his embrace so much. His discipline was sexy, no doubt about it. Knowing her inclinations and his powers, she deflected the visible rays of attraction.

"So tell me about this picture."

"That picture, Ms. Elyse, is of my great-great-grandmother in her twenties."

"Lovely," she admired softly. The woman in the photograph was a beautiful picture of life in the world of couture. Not only did her caramel skin, striking pose, and brown doe-inspired eyes make her look like a Harlem goddess, but she wore a bold seductive facial expression to accent her elaborate satin-like dress. Her bosom was projected in pride, left hand on her hip and right behind her head slightly tilted back. The antique goddess was inspiring and invigorating.

"She was an amazing woman. Her name was Ethel Mason. Singer and entertainer."

"She must have had an exciting life," she replied, examining the picture.

"Is that a wedding ring on her finger?"

"Not quite. She received that ring from a white slave owner. They were in love."

Elyse turned from the picture. She was trying to process Malcolm's explanation, but nothing was creating a quick computation. Finally her mouth caught up to her brain's digestion. "They were in love?"

"Yes."

Waiting for more, Elyse petitioned the goddess's history. "Do you mind sharing details?"

He laughed at her curiosity, but was flattered to satisfy it. "Sure. I figured that 'yes' wouldn't suffice."

"You know me."

"At least a little bit, anyway," he replied with a smile. "Her singing charmed the heart of a slave owner sitting in the audience one night. He was so entranced by her that he asked her to spend a night with him. She obliged his request and he occasionally came up to see her shows. He offered to create a life for her at his plantation house with the promise that she wouldn't have to work another day in her life. She didn't take his proposition, but thinking she was just playing hard to get, he gave her a ring to remember him by."

"Hmm," she listened intently. "That's an amazing story."

"It gets better. A couple of years passed. He traveled to see her again and proposed the same offer. My great-great-grandmother was still wearing the ring in that picture, yet she still turned him down."

Hanging on his last words, she noticed his pause, but craved more of the history behind the frame. "Why?" she asked anxiously.

"She was saving money to leave a legacy for her children. She said she valued her freedom to work and that the night before wasn't worth the morning after. That there's always a morning after, no matter what your life looks like at night. No matter what, you have to deal with your decision the next day. I've tried to live by that. She kept the ring because she loved him, but she kept working because she loved herself."

Elyse just stared at him in amazement of what her eyes were beholding. She was looking at the fruits of Ms. Mason's labor of love. And conviction.

"The morning after," she repeated, holding the picture in her hands.

"That's a definite message. Something I've never thought of."

"Yeah, that picture has spoken volumes even though she's gone." Elyse ran her fingertips across Ms. Mason's ring and let her mantra resonate within her on the way home.

CHAPTER 9

Elyse found herself gazing into a deep abyss of heavy oblivion. She stared at the neutral-colored walls of her office, fixated on the thoughts floating to the surface of her consciousness. A train could have rolled between her and the imaginary dot on the wall and she wouldn't have broken her concentration. Her eyes were glazed with wishful thinking and recollection as she remembered that she loved to paint, draw, and color in coloring books; loved to make mud pies; loved to stare into night skies and imagine what aliens looked like on Jupiter. She thought of her mother's smile and it trickled down from the spiritual realm onto her lips, causing them to curve in a similar fashion. She thought of the former "where I want to be when I'm twenty" goals she wrote in middle school and that she used to be giddy coifing her friends' ponytails, pretending to shampoo, condition, and dry their hair in her imaginary salon. She often wondered what happened to them after they parted ways. She hated that she had to move away, but it was inevitable. Her father was an ambassador for change in underdeveloped countries. His extensive travel meant saving the lives of innocent people, yet it also meant the uprooting of her life at any given moment. She appreciated his philanthropic passion, which ran deep in her veins. She loved playing soccer in Kenya and eating candied jalapeños in Mexico City. She pondered the possibility of obtaining a pilot's license so she could fly away whenever the hell she wanted. Then she smiled again at the thought of herself in a plane, in a fair blue sky sprayed with white puffs of cotton-candy clouds. Her eyelids met one another and she inhaled the fresh air in her mind. Elyse continued down the paisley path of a-little-bit-of-everything-ness. There were flowers on her right and left, brightly facing her as she walked freely in her psyche. Then one of them opened its mouth and said "Ms. Adams." She walked further and another flower opened its mouth and made a noise like a muffled fire alarm. It closed its mouth, smiled at her, and opened it again with the same annoying sound. She blinked softly into reality and the neutral-colored wall in her office that was once translucent began to blur, then her eyes focused and it all turned clear. Her eyes shifted to the doorway to find her assistant standing there. Her cell phone was ringing, hence the weird sounding flower.

"Ms. Adams, your four o'clock is here," said Trey. "Would you like me to send him in?"

She looked at the clock on her desktop. It was 3:17. She had been in a daze for what seemed like forever, but it was only 3 minutes long. A bit taken off guard, Elyse answered, "Sure, send him in."

Trey hurried off to the front of the atrium to retrieve her appointment. Meanwhile, Elyse shifted the array of papers next to her standing file folders. She forwarded her office and cell phone to voicemail and minimized the programs on her computer screen. Her four o'clock appointment strolled in bright-eyed and with a huge smile on his face.

"Elyse."

She stood to greet him properly, extending her hand. "Malcolm," she answered. "How has your day been?"

"Great. Busy. You know me," he said, shaking her hand.

"I'll take your word for it that you were actually busy and not fooling around with God's time."

"Wow! We're taking it *there* today," Malcolm said grinning. "I think I use God's time quite wisely, but I'm sure you would say something differently."

"Well, I can't be the judge of that, so let's just get down to business," she replied. "How can I assist you today?"

"You can assist me by accompanying me to dinner after you get off work."

"Is that the pertinent business at hand?"

"Absolutely."

"You've *got* to be kidding."

"No, I'm not."

"You made an appointment at my office to ask me out to dinner in a few hours," Elyse repeated, trying to grasp the rationale.

"You didn't return my phone calls this week."

Shifting the papers from one side of the desk to the other, she tried not to look flattered.

"I didn't deem it necessary to respond quickly, plus, I've really been busy."

Malcolm tilted his head slightly to the right. "Oh, really? That's sad."

"And why is that sad?" Elyse inquired.

"Because you could have missed out on a beautiful experience."

"So you're just offering *one* per lifetime?" she asked him sarcastically.

He looked into her eyes and thought of the first night he indulged her. Then he fast-forwarded to her sitting in the office, looking deliciously inviting in her tailored charcoal grey suit and amethyst French-cuffed dress shirt. Her thin box chain necklace was home to a gold slightly-curved leaf charm, subliminally suggesting to his eyes to slide down the imaginary pleasure path between her breasts. How beautiful she was the night they were together, and how desirable she was now, clothed. He thought to himself, "I can offer more than that in your lifetime if you let me." She placed her hand between his field of vision and her chest, and then pointed upward to her face. He bit his lip, thinking of her fingertips running down his spine. Then his eyes lifted slowly to her chin, then to her lips, her nose, finally resting upon her eyes.

"Focus," she commanded with fortitude.

"I was," he answered with a smile.

She briefly paused to derail her perception of his thought pattern. She took a quick deep breath and summoned a purpose out of his cup of flirtation.

"So, Mr. Harrison, why are you here, *still* in my office?"

He straightened up in her office chair, but his intentions were not shaken. He wasn't leaving without another date.

"Well, Ms. Adams, I proposed a dinner offer quite earlier in this conversation. You haven't presented an answer. Here's my final offer and I'm not accepting no for answer." He slid a note card embossed with his initials across her desk. Elyse looked at him, expecting inked foolishness. When she reached for the note, Malcolm placed his hand over hers to interject a caution.

"I must warn you. The current offer you are about to read is being presented with sincerity and by no means indicates that we are a couple or that I want sex from you in return."

Elyse laughed at his frankness and shook her head. "Shut up and give me the note."

Malcolm continued, "Or that you are indebted to receive said offer as a result of your unfortunate running incident last week. Do you understand the contents of this disclaimer?" Reviewing contracts were like reading nursery rhymes to him. In this case, being a car salesman had its advantages.

She mentally called him pitiful then shook her head, "Just give me the note."

He released her hand and added an *okay, suit yourself* gesture as she turned over the card to read his offer. The card read:

> *Join me Saturday morning at 9 o'clock at*
> *The Prime Café on 23rd Street and Grayson for*
> *a sample of my immaculate cooking skills.*
> *If you are disappointed, which is highly*
> *unlikely, I will be forced to more pathetic*
> *measures of requesting your presence in mine.*

Elyse glanced over the note again, reading the first sentence slowly before revisiting the second. The Prime Café was the only establishment that offered its patrons the option of making breakfast for their party, adding whatever tasting preferences their guests desired. It was a cozy, yet classy café adorned with bookshelves, pastry trays, and work from local artists, which made for a comfortable atmosphere both for morning and evening engagements. Kin took her there on a spontaneous date once, and she remembered the smell of hot chocolate, mocha latte, and éclairs sprinkled with brown sugar. The memories put a smile on her face and Malcolm knew she had accepted his offer.

"So I'll pick you up at 8:30?" He asked, standing up from the grey office chair.

"Wait, I didn't accept your offer and this isn't dinner, it's breakfast."

"You haven't refused, so it's a date," he answered, picking up his umbrella resting against the wall.

Her mouth opened in disbelief and no words flowed from her lips to confirm or deny his statement.

"See? You accept." He smiled and turned to exit. "I'll pick you up at 8:30. Wear that beautiful skin, alright?"

"Wait!" Elyse walked from behind her desk and over to the threshold of her office. She looked at his face in amazement of his tactic, then grabbed a pen from her desk and wrote on the note card away from his sight. She placed the note card in his jacket pocket, affirming that it was at the base of its seam. After closing the pocket flap, she managed to gather some words for his whirlwind of assertiveness.

"Check my response when you get home. I don't want you to get too emotional."

"Sure. Have a great evening, Ms. Adams." Nonchalantly and chipper, he walked away.

"Same to you, Mr. Harrison."

Malcolm spoke cordially to her assistant on his way to the elevator lobby. The piece of paper was burning a hole in his suit jacket, and in his mind. There was a rounded tone as the downward arrow button light went dim. The elevator door opened and he proceeded forward. "Wait until I get home," he thought. He pressed "1" and the rounded tone sounded once more as the door closed. He reached in his pocket for the note card and flipped it over to find a big "OK" written across his words, with a smiley face inserted in the "O" plus another line he wasn't expecting: "Meet you there." He nodded in honor of her request and was relieved that she had accepted at all. The most important thing was he had a breakfast date with the woman of his intentions, and he tried his best to curb his enthusiasm and relief as he walked from the elevator to the building entrance and to his car.

***

The Prime Café was a beautiful date suggestion, as its bricked entrance was decorated with a mixture of fresh flowers, including brightly planted gerbera daisies, plus the smell of freshly-baked bread and honey pancakes could be detected blocks away. Elyse parked her silver convertible in the parking lot and inhaled deeply. Then she exhaled with delight. She hadn't been to The Prime since the separation and it felt good to begin to enjoy it all over again. The beads of sweat on her right hand indicated a bit of nervousness and apprehension, but she turned off the ignition and carried her purse inside the café. She walked in, not looking for Malcolm, but looking for familiarity. There was still a picture of Nelson Mandela on the right-hand wall and a picture of

Josephine Baker on the left. They had changed the window dressings to a burnt orange mandarin silk. It was light, inviting, and gave the café a warm sunrise glow. A vintage advertisement reading *"Chocolat 5 cents"* was panoramically placed over the bookcases. Elyse looked up to find ceiling fan blades shaped like coffee beans whirling above her head. The smell of breakfast filled her soul. Her eyes lay upon the table in the right-hand corner where she and Kin used to sit. It was empty. "This is ridiculous. It's a table with chairs, Lys. Just sit down." She made her feet walk forward in order to attempt to jump over her nostalgia, which concluded in her sitting at that very table. She placed her purse in the chair next to her and looked at her watch. It was 8:49.

"Good Morning, Ms. Adams! It's great to see you again. Would you like your usual?"

Actually she had almost forgotten what her usual was. "No thank you, Yvette. I have a meeting here at nine. I'll just wait until my party arrives. How's school?"

"Going fine. I'm in my sophomore year at Fisk now, so it's moving along," answered Yvette. "Um, Ms. Adams, I don't mean to intrude, but does your party include Mr. Malcolm Harrison?"

"You're not intruding, Yvette, but I do wonder why you ask."

"Because he scheduled a breakfast session this morning at nine and said that it was for a special guest. He described you and I was wondering...if..." Yvette was choked for words and Elyse decided to ease her discomfort.

"You were wondering if I was meeting Mr. Morton," she responded nicely.

Yvette looked down at the Fisk University pin on her café uniform apron. "Yes ma'am. I didn't want you to think I was being nosey."

Elyse took Yvette's nervous hand and held it softly. "Yvette, I've known you since you were thirteen and in my sister's English class. It's okay to ask. And the answer is no. Mr. Morton and I are no longer together. You're fine."

"Thanks," she replied with relief. "I'll be back to check on you later, okay?"

"Okay, sweetie," smiled Elyse. Yvette had grown to a young woman, and out of everyone she had spoken to for the last year, she was the first person to whom Elyse had verbalized the divorce after its finality. Simply put, it felt weird for the words to leave her lips, although they were true.

Elyse looked out of the window pane and found her composure floating in the air. She was proud of herself for making it this far and not crumbling as she did when the unwanted ball started rolling.

8:56.

"He'd better not be late," she muttered to her watch.

She looked in her purse for a pen and notepad to write a thought. As she placed the tip of the pen on the paper, the thought flowed, beginning with the following:

I am equipped to handle this. I will not sink. I am beautiful and resilient. I am human and I was born to outlive my fear. There are some things I will be able to jump over and some that I will have to go through and fear will always be waiting for me on the other side. I choose to outlive my fear today.

She shifted her weight in her seat and spilled more thoughts on the notepad's page.

Every now and then, it helps to remind you of whose you are, Elyse, and that you are an evolving piece of art, not a stagnant piece of stone. And even stone is permeable, so how invincible are we to change? Changing is good. Embrace it.

When she wrote the last word for the moment, she realized that she was sitting a bit straighter than she was when she entered the café.

"Having fun over there, Scribe?" Malcolm asked her, coming from the kitchen's door.

She smiled. "Yes I am, sir. Thank you. And how long have you been here? I was starting to think you stood me up."

"Never that, at least not intentionally. I've been here for almost an hour, preparing for you."

"Well, I must say. You do look cute in that black apron. I assume the food will be delectable as promised."

"*As promised* is correct, and I keep my promises. Do you have any allergies?"

"No, I'm good. Thanks."

"Great. I was hoping not. I used special ingredients in the crepes."

"Crepes?" Elyse slowly tilted her head and shoulders back in shock.

"Yeah! Crepes!" he confirmed emphatically. "You know those thin pancakes invented by the French? They're usually topped with…"

"I know what crepes are, Genius. I just didn't think you could prepare them…properly. My father cooked them when we visited Nice. I don't know if you're going to top that."

"Thanks, I'll take that as a challenge," said Malcolm. "So, are you ready? I hope you brought your appetite."

"You're NOT welcome. Yes, I'm ready and yes I did."

He flashed that dimpled smile at her again. His warmth radiated through it, so much so that she had to make a conscious effort to pull her eyes back to meet his and not stare at his perfectly straight teeth. He winked at her and she tried her best not to smile back like a giddy schoolgirl receiving attention from the captain of the football team. He motioned for her to put away her pen and pad. "Well, let's get to it. I hope you love every bite."

There was something about Malcolm that made her comfortable with adventure. Comfortable with the unknown. Comfortable in knowing that she was secure in wherever he led her. She couldn't put her finger on it either. That was new, since she read him like a book when they met at Delilah's. At any rate of speed this was going, she was getting used to this new level of comfort with him—a far cry from her conservative and feminist values. It felt good not to think, create, and problem-solve with every encounter. To be able to sit in the passenger's seat on a romantic journey and let someone else drive was an exhilarating experience that she could recall few and far between in her past relationships. This was something she could get used to permanently if the opportunity presented itself. Elyse tried not to transfer Kin's abusive scars onto this new canvas, but she was a work in progress. After all, this was how they started their courtship too—learning each other by experiencing new things together. Without letting Malcolm see her cobwebs of thought, she lightly shook her head to knock them out of their corners. One thing was for sure, she was loving breakfast. She was enjoying the sound of her laughter. It sounded like freedom. That feeling of joy was as appetizing as Malcolm's cinnamon crepes and she couldn't wait to experience more.

***

"Two cold ones?"

"Um, sure. I didn't know you were a drinker," he said, taken aback.

She reached into the refrigerator and pulled out two bottles of water. She held up the bottlenecks with her right hand poking fun at his alcoholic expectation.

"Good one," Malcolm said laughing and scratching his temple.

"Looks like you're feeling better."

"I am. Definitely better than last week, thanks to your bedside manner," Elyse said sincerely. "I truly appreciate everything."

"My pleasure. Just glad to see you back. So when's the next time we're working out? Monday?"

"Um, no, I think I'll pass. I've had enough of your rigorous training. You're a little serious." She took a sip of her cold water.

"I'm not as laborious as you think. Promise," he assured her, smiling. "Your body was exhausted *before* the workout. You stretched it too far and it crashed. I didn't do anything to facilitate that process. Your passing out was inevitable."

"Inevitable, huh?"

"That's right. Inevitable. Bound to happen sooner or later. You really should think about taking it easy more often. When's the last time you had a vacation?"

"I take time for myself, thank you. I just didn't get much sleep the last couple of weeks."

"You didn't answer my question."

"The last time I had a vacation was a little over a year ago. And it was fabulous." She sipped more water from her bottle. His smile was making her a little heated and she was desperately trying to do her part to maintain the "starting over" principle they agreed upon.

"That's nice. What did you do?" he questioned. He sensed she was skimming around the truth and decided to catch her on the next lap of her ice-skating exhibition.

"Some girlfriends and I went to Las Vegas last year. Had an absolute ball."

"That's great! Did you see some shows, gamble, and dine at some restaurants?"

Elyse took another sip of water.

"Did you meet some cool people? Did you swim in any of the indoor pools? What about a spa treatment. I know you took a trip to the spa while you were there."

She swallowed a couple of swigs in the attempt to quench her sexual urges.

"Did you do anything while you were in the City of Sin?"

Her wrist tipped the water bottle towards her mouth once more, but she missed it and the water dripped on her shirt. Taking the cue, Malcolm interjected.

"You know there is such thing as drinking too much water at one time. Do you turn into a mermaid at night or something?"

"What happens in Vegas..." she smiled coyly.

Her facial expression was what he was looking for to break the ice. He remembered the conversation he and his mother had and decided to ask Elyse to attend church with him. He drank more water to calm his own adrenaline. His nervousness was moving through his body like wildfire. "Why am I so nervous? It's just church," he psyched himself up; however, he knew what the deal really was. She was not only going to church with him, she was meeting his mother for the first time. To cushion the possible blow, he decided to preface it with a general conversation.

"So how do you feel about church?"

Elyse almost choked on her water. "What?"

"How do you feel about church? Do you attend one around here?"

She looked at him puzzled and slightly offended. Did she look like a heathen to him? Sure, they had slept together, but the question seemed to fall from the middle of the ceiling. "Where did that come from?" she asked, attempting to get straight to the source of his inquisition.

"No reason, I just thought I'd ask before inviting you to mine."

"So now you ask around what you really want to know? You didn't do that when you asked me out at Delilah's."

Malcolm sat a little straighter and took another swig of his bottled water. He sucked it so hard, it made a loud pop when he released it. Elyse seized the opportunity to continue her point of view.

"Plus, I don't do church anyway. I just don't do it. I used to go to church when I was a little girl, and it was hell. One of the deacons fondled me while I was in the baptismal pool and I never fit in with the congregation. They were always talking about other people sitting a few pews in front of them. The hugs were fake and they came to church just for drama and gossip." Elyse took a sip and nonchalantly continued, "When my mother died, my father stopped going.

Eventually, my sister and I stopped going also. I don't see the point of going back. I know God, I pray, and I read my Bible when I can. So, why should I go to church with a bunch of actors?"

Malcolm was stunned by her response. He had stood on the railroad tracks and didn't realize that the E-Train was coming full speed ahead. Regret and sorrow filled his heart as he retraced the steps of her conversation.

"I'm sorry you were molested, Elyse. That was unacceptable. That shouldn't have happened to you. I don't know what to say."

She finished off her water with a streak of numbness. "It's okay. Everything happens for a reason. It was just difficult going to church knowing he would be there watching me. For a long time, I told my mom that I didn't want to wear dresses to church. I just didn't want to tease him or give him any ideas."

"Elyse, you're an attractive woman, but no man should be looking at a little girl in that way. It was wrong and you had nothing to do with it. You didn't tease him. It's not your fault. He was wrong and it shouldn't have happened."

She played with the label on the empty water bottle. "I know. That and the other stuff that followed just killed church for me, that's all." Malcolm held his hand out, palm up. Elyse accepted and placed her hand in his.

"Thank you for telling me. I understand you're not interested in going to any church, not just mine. If it helps, my mother wants you to come to fellowship and eat with us afterwards. She's excited to meet you. To her, it's a way of sharing that excitement with other people who are dear to her, like a family gathering."

Elyse screwed and unscrewed the bottle top robotically. She wanted to accept upon flattery alone, but her mind was telling her that was a bad idea. Her professional instincts kicked in and she quickly weighed the pros and cons silently.

Meeting Malcolm's mother
– PRO

Sitting next to Malcolm and his mother
– PRO-MAYBE

Weird looks from the clergy
- CON

Standing for recognition of visitors
– CON

Fake smiles from people looking at clothes and shoes
– CON

"I can tell you're thinking, and that's okay," Malcolm reassured her. "I know you don't need saving, but just so you know in your heart, I'll be right there. I won't leave you. Nothing will happen to you on my watch and you'll be by my side the entire time. I'll even protect you from the police... I mean, my mother's friends."

She smiled at his effort. "Thanks for the offer, but like I said, church really isn't my thing. I would still like to have dinner with your mother though. Maybe we can start there."

It wasn't the answer he wanted to hear, but he couldn't force this grown woman to do anything she didn't want to do; however, her voice resembled a vulnerable little girl looking outside of the porch screen door. He could tell that she wanted to come, but wasn't quite ready to be submerged into that world.

"And for the record, I was sick with a stomach virus the entire week in Vegas. I was in bed the majority of the trip. Miserable."

CHAPTER 10

Driving at night, the moon looked like a glowing powdered sugar cookie, half-eaten after being dunked in a glass of milk. The edges were brushed as if a fine-tooth comb had coifed them. In the driver's seat of her sister's SUV, Elyse experienced the culmination of the most convenient part of being a childless aunt—returning her niece to her parents after a weekend of fun, food, and the circus. In a way, she and Kaye were a lot alike. Both females had relatively short attention spans and enjoyed action movies. Both were solution-focused and fiercely loved the colors pink and purple. Both also prized the leaf charms around their necks.

When an Adams baby was born, she or he was celebrated with a ceremonial baby dedication and a lively reception at the parents' home. The new addition to the family was bestowed a treasured leaf charm to welcome them to the tribe. It was a proud family tradition dating back from the 1920's that kept the Adamses a cohesive unit despite hard times. Gold leaves were given to baby boys to remind them that they would be tested immensely during their journey towards manhood. Being a soft metal, gold signified that being an Adams man meant being the opposite of society's standards. He was expected to exhibit fervor in achieving his goals, but be malleable when necessary. He could not afford to be emotionless and stagnant as the future head of his family and community. The baby girls' leaf charms were made of silver, a softer metal, but great conductor of heat and electricity. It was a reminder for them to be resilient despite society's expectation for them to be conforming and succumbing. Each girl would learn that their femininity was not a weakness, but a strength. As Elyse looked in the rear view mirror at the flicker of light dancing on Kaye's leaf charm, she was reminded how far their family had come, how much strength had come through their lineage, and how bright their future looked with Kaye's curious mind.

"How come the moon is following us, Auntie Lys?" asked the now five-year-old Kaye, gazing upwards to her right-backseat window.

"Why?"

Kaye sighed in annoyance. "*Why* is the moon following us, Auntie Lys?"

"From our point of view, it just seems like the moon is following us, Sweetie. It's really goes in a circle around the Earth."

"But I thought the Earth goes around the sun. How can it go around us?"

"Boy, your mama's summer homeschooling sessions really did work. Who knew?" she thought. "Well, Earth goes in a circle around the sun, like you said. While we go around the sun, the moon goes around us in a smaller circle. Both of us go around the sun together."

Elyse looked into her rearview mirror for confirmation of understanding. Kaye blinked at her, then looked at the moon, then at her again.

"So the moon is our buddy, like we're the sun's buddy," Kaye summarized.

"Right! That's a good way to think of it. Good job, Smart Girl!"

"Yayyyyy, Kaayyyyyeee!!!!" she screamed from her car seat, clapping her hands.

"Yayyyy, Kaye!" Elyse agreed with a smile.

***

When she arrived at the Petersons' home, Elyse noticed that it took extra time for her sister and Lenn to answer the door.

"What's taking them so long?" she asked Kaye rhetorically.

"Maybe they're wrestling."

Elyse shot a look down to the half-pint genius holding her hands. She didn't even want to know how her sister explained her escapades with Lenn to her niece.

"Get the hell out of my house, Leo-nard!"

Knowing that Shara only called Lenn by his government name when things got bad, she calmly looked for her emergency house key in her purse. She didn't want to startle Kaye, but she knew it wasn't going to be long before her little mind would form a hypothesis about the moment. Then came the sound of crashing glass. She could tell the sound was coming from upstairs. Elyse dug a little deeper to locate the key at the bottom of her purse.

"Auntie Lys?"

"Yes, Baby?"

"I'm scared." Kaye's concerned eyes cracked the methodical nature of Elyse's mind for a moment. She knew what she had to do first. Kneeling down in front of her, she grabbed both Kaye's hands and smiled.

"It's okay, Sweetheart. We're going to go inside and you're going to immediately sit on the couch in the living room while I go check everything out, okay? You have your e-game in your book bag and your headphones. Do Auntie Lys a favor and put on your headphones as soon as you get inside so you can play your e-game and beat your latest score. I'll come downstairs and get you so we can go to my house for another night of ice cream and movies. Mommy and Daddy need to be alone tonight and we're going to help them do that. Okay, Smart Girl?"

"Yes, Ma'am. I want to help."

"I know you do and you're doing a great job of helping them right now. So, let's go inside and remember what I told you."

Kaye nodded her head and Elyse affirmed. She didn't know what they were about to walk into, but she knew they couldn't just walk away. After all, her sister could be in danger and leaving her in a volatile situation was not an option, no matter whose fault it was.

She opened the door and Kaye rushed in to sit on the couch to complete her instructions. Elyse reached back to press the doorbell repeatedly to give the alert that she was coming in. She locked the door behind her and walked calmly upstairs. Kaye's eyes followed her aunt's swift motion up the staircase. She quickly looked back at her e-game and turned up the volume.

"Why would you do this to us, you son-of-a..." Shara screamed.

"Don't you dare say that to me! You and I both know who the real bitch is in this house!" Lenn hollered back.

"I can show you that right now!" she retorted as she sprang forward like a track star at the sound of the gun. Elyse opened the door to their bedroom and found Shara and Lenn tousling around on the floor like grade school kids. There were scattered pornographic magazines on the bed and the floor. His cell phone was shattered on the bed and their commemorative glass wedding vase was in pieces next to their wedding picture. Elyse quickly put the pieces of the fight together and sprang into action.

"STOP! YOUR DAUGHTER IS HERE!"

Shara and Lenn wrestled with more intensity. The scenario was not uncommon since they were both athletes in college and would wrestle each other for fun. It would usually lead to them having explosive sex afterward, and Elyse always got the earful of what happened the night before on her cell phone. But this time, there was anger in both of their spirits, dancing with charms around his wrists, enticing them to block out everything she said.

"KAYE! IS! HEEEERRRRE!" Elyse shouted from above their heads. Shara was on top of him now, but Lenn had arrested her hands to prevent her from slapping him again.

They stopped like deer in headlights staring at the truth they just heard. Breathing heavily like animals, they untangled their web of physical rage and slowly stood up. Shara took the opportunity to push Lenn one more good time.

"You're going to create images for your daughter that you can't erase and I can't keep covering for you two! You've never been this bad! This is CRAZY! What is really going on?"

"Kaye's *father*," Shara emphasized with a sassy neck roll and glaring look at Lenn, "has taken it upon himself to bring this mess into our house! These magazines, the text messages, he even has a webcam in the bathroom! THE BATHROOM! What am I supposed to do about this? I can't live with a man that can't control his own urges around his family. I can't continue to…to…*sponsor* this foolishness! I've done everything I could to make sure that everything stays running around here. That the bills get paid, that Kaye gets off to school okay. And I come home and find this thing in the bathroom?!" Shara held up the wires to the webcam that she had ripped out from the wall. "I just can't do this anymore." She threw up her hands, instinctively opened her palms to release the wires, and walked out of the bedroom. Her pounding footsteps alarmed Kaye and their eyes briefly met at the top of the staircase. Shara woke up out of her feeling of desperation, returned quietly to the bedroom, and closed the door carefully.

"Something's got to give. For real. And I think it's going to be me." Lenn's words confused both of the Adams girls in the room as he took off his wedding band. "I'm going to get myself together and I can't be with you while I do it."

Elyse stood confused and scared. Her sister and her brother-in-law had been her role model of the perfect marriage until Lenn lost his job. Things seemed to go south quickly after that change.

He put the wedding band on the disheveled bed and stared at Shara for confirmation. He never took off his ring, even when he applied lotion on his hands. He simply would wipe it off afterward to make it shine again. This time, Shara knew his spirit was for real. She took a time-traveling gaze into his soul and saw the man she married. The ambitious architect, the loving father, the mind-blowing lover. He wasn't a weak-minded fool anymore; he was real. A real sculpture of imperfection trying to cure the illness of feeling incompetent. She knew she couldn't compete with his mind. It was made and it was clear.

***

When she returned home, Elyse opened the cover of her red leather journal, grabbed her black fountain pen and began to release her thoughts:

It's amazing how the younger we are, the less tangible our fears are. We're afraid of scary movie characters and toilets flushings but curious of waterbugs and airline flights. No fear of heights or tragic disasters, just enjoying the ride and looking down. When did we cross that threshold of fear? Fearing the big and the little stuff? Fearing heights?? We used to jump off of things all of the time. Height was never an issue. If anything, someone had to stop us from jumping from such ridiculously high platforms, like high porches and banisters. We would just look at it and say "I bet you can't jump off of that!" and the response, oh-so-proper was, "Oh yes I can!" With so much authority, tenacity, and assurance, we answered the call to action AND followed through with it! Where did that go? Why don't we do that now? That fiery, passionate confidence that said, "I can do this! Just watch me!" seemed to have shrunken due to adult responsibilities, infringements upon our freedom, and dark gaping holes of pain induced by ourselves and others. We need that confidence again when we're adults. That self-confirmation that propels us so aggressively toward our mark, shoots us across negativity and through all our self-inflicted brick walls. So after jumping from the high porch, we hurt our knees, ankles, and hands. But if we don't get hurt, we can get up smiling hard because we did it and would do it again if challenged. I love that spirit. Reminds me that I don't have all the time in world to live my life. I really need to jump, but it looks so high...

She dropped her pen between the pages and closed the journal. The sound of the central air conditioning unit dominated in the background as she walked toward her bedroom. One last look out of the window and she saw the moon shining on the leaves outside. Elyse thought of her niece and their conversation in the car. Perhaps God could send her a satellite so she could reflect His light a little brighter at work tomorrow and coruscate to other areas in her life as well. With that thought, she prayed, asking God to let her be a little more like her niece and accept His plan with Kaye's type of innocence and trust. She prayed a little while longer before rising to her feet. She had a feeling she was going to need it soon. Before she could drift into slumber, the phone rang. It was 10:30 at night and Malcolm usually called before the evening news. When she answered his call, she could tell something had been weighing on his mind—

church. She couldn't understand why her attendance at church was so important to him, as if he were a spokesperson of the "everybody should go to church" club. Despite her feelings, she gave into his request. On the other end of the phone, Malcolm was relieved to hear her response, even at such short notice. Elyse hung up the phone and rolled over. Then, she looked up towards heaven and gave God "the eye".

"I guess that's what the extra prayer was for," she said before groaning in angst over Sunday morning's adventure and closing her eyes for the night.

***

Malcolm and Elyse arrived at church at 10:45, fifteen minutes before service began. As they proceeded to the door, his church members greeted him with hugs and salutations. Elyse smiled in the background and tried not to show her discomfort. She was determined to stay open and friendly throughout the entire experience. She figured if she treated it like a business meeting, she would pass with flying colors.

The music was nice, but what pulled her heartstrings was a little boy who appeared to be about nine years of age. He was singing in the choir stand next to his mother, rocking from side to side and clapping his hands with fervor and joy. He looked so happy to be there, and when it was his turn to lead a song, he sung it with all of his might, although off-key. Elyse was amazed at how no one seemed to mind all of the discordant notes. Instead, people were clapping, smiling, and encouraging him to sing his heart out. She couldn't believe what she was seeing—seemingly nice people. After the song was over, there was a great applause and overwhelming urge to stand up and ask for another selection. A deacon rose to his feet and proceeded to the podium while ushers brought offering plates to the front of the church.

"Great, here comes the offering," she mumbled. Malcolm decided to let her slide as he knew the origins of her pessimistic statement. Shara was the benevolent person in the family, just like her mother. She would give the shirt and shoes she wore if someone truly needed it. She gave without a second thought. Elyse, on the other hand, was the opposite. She wasn't exactly Scrooge, but she was very careful in giving offerings and donations. She never trusted deacons and preachers to be right-standing when it came to money and power. When the deacon read the verse about being a cheerful giver, she could not easily gainsay it. That was one of her mantras: if you give something, give it because you want to. She placed $5.00 in the collection plate and smiled in pride because it was more than a dollar. Her heart was actually warming to the church. Its loving atmosphere was contagious. Her smiles appeared more frequently, even when she wasn't trying. When time came for the sermon, she felt sleepy. Malcolm occasionally nudged her and embarrassment overshadowed her enjoyment. The minister's message was far from boring and she was desperately trying to tune in to his channel.

Then, suddenly the frequency of the pastor's voice seemed to break through her narcoleptic shell with one word—forgiveness. She heard it, but there was depth to his version of the concept.

"Forgiveness has a root word that indicates that it is a gift," the pastor explained. "The word 'for' indicates going beyond the distance of giving or releasing something to someone without the expectation of getting paid for it. To for-give means to complete this act of giving with intense, proactive force. You forewarn someone before the moment a usual warning would take place. You forecast the weather days ahead of schedule. To forgive implies that pardon is released before the apology. To say that you for-give someone, you have given a pardon that you cannot take back. Forgiveness is a permanent exchange, not a reversible transaction. The fact that it is a gift also means that it will cost you something to let it go."

Elyse felt her heart tugging at each example that followed the exegesis of the text he chose. He walked through the life of Job forgiving his friends after they mocked and left him, Stephen forgiving his stone throwers moments before he died at their hands, and Jesus forgiving his accusers as He died on the cross at Golgotha. Elyse had heard these stories before, but never had they been so clear. Never had their historical courage made so much sense to her current conniption. She had to forgive Kin. She had to forgive herself. And most importantly, she had to allow God to forgive her.

***

Once service ended, there was the usual chatter and fellowship in the hallways and vestibule as members trickled out of the door toward their cars. Malcolm made a point to hold her hand in each inquisitive encounter with his church family, and she tightly accepted his security. Her hands were sweaty, but he didn't care. She was vulnerable—finally—and he appreciated her trust.

They walked by a living wall garden surrounding a brick rectangle hosting a plaque made of brass. It was lovely. Elyse was eager to learn of the name etched in honor.

"She was known as Mother Johnson. Her husband, Eddie Lee, was the Sunday School superintendent. They were well loved throughout the community and highly devoted to this church," Malcolm disclosed. "She raped me during Sunday School one morning. Told me that having sex with her was the way to show God's love, in so many words. I was six. I didn't know any better and I didn't want God to be mad at me, so..."

He lowered his eyes in respect for the dead and in preparation for what was flowing from his heart unexpectedly.

"She touched me. I touched her. I did what she told me to and it looked like she was happy so I didn't think it was wrong. Then she screamed. I'll never forget that sound. It scared me, but she told me to keep going; that God made my hands the perfect size. To hear her say that made me feel good about myself and she made me feel like I was helping her."

He paused and looked at his right hand. Elyse wanted to shoot every live wire in her nerves to stop them from screaming at her. Instinctively, she wanted to let go of his hand after knowing its story, but chose to hold it all the more. Sweat and all.

"That Sunday night, I kept staring at my hands. They felt so dirty. I washed them over and over again in the church bathroom to get rid of the smell," he shared, looking up at the plaque. "I couldn't explain it, but I wanted to do it again. I want to make her feel better. So, this was a regular thing when she babysat me at her home. At one point, I don't know why, but I finally felt uncomfortable with the invisible dirt on my hands and the odor it left behind. I was so confused. I had no idea what to tell my parents. So I didn't. I didn't tell anyone. I came to church, and she gave me candy to keep my mouth shut. I stayed quiet about the whole thing until she died at age fifty-four. Kidney disease. They dedicated this wall in her honor and made a big donation to the Alabama Kidney Foundation."

Elyse took a deep breath, but carefully exhaled slowly as to not disturb his confession. She simply couldn't believe that the same man that carried her home after their workout had once housed a crumbling little boy with the need for validation and esteem. He was amazing to behold and she had never seen a man be so human. Mr. Adams was a battle ax. Forged and fortified with all things manly. Kin was no different in all of his athletic glory. There was no such thing as vulnerability in either household from the masculine end of the spectrum.

"I couldn't walk by here for years," Malcolm acknowledged. "Then, forgiveness became a necessity instead of an option in order for me to live outside of her chains. I had to love me more than I hated her. I had to let her go, Elyse. Completely. She was dead. And there was no way to receive her apology. I had no choice but to for-*give* her."

He stared at Mother Johnson's name and raised his left hand to touch it, lightly patting it once like a silent amen before letting it slowly slide down the living wall of plant life. Elyse reached out to meet his open soul with her right hand. She had an overwhelming desire to cover his nakedness starting with his shoulders. She saw the strength of his heart beating through his words and the authenticity of his care through actions. She was on board. A diving board straight into his spirit. And it surpassed the sex and the romantic dinners. It led straight to the bottom of his oceanic love. They stood in front of the wall as the church seemed to scatter around them in slow motion. There they were, standing in a holy place, in their humanity and in love, in the morning after, at the same time.

CHAPTER 11

I took her back."

An inquisitive Elyse squinted her eyes for more information. She felt slightly offended. William felt the flames starting to crackle from her eyes, but kept looking down at the new environmental codes implemented by the city council.

"You took her back." Elyse repeated, standing in front of his office door.

William looked up from the papers. "Yes, I took her back."

Elyse, still confused at the outcome, managed to make her eyes blink into reality. Whatever reason she was about to hear wasn't good enough for her to see Rachel in a redeemable light. William scribbled on the top page and tucked it under the stack. He began skimming over the next page as if his answer was enough.

"William."

He sighed and paused his autopilot mode.

"Yes, Elyse."

"Are you going to tell me what's going on or what?"

"Am I going to tell you? I just did. She cheated. I kicked her out. She apologized. I let her back in. Case closed."

"Case closed?" Elyse sternly asked. "In a situation like this, it's hardly case closed that fast. There's more to this story than what you're telling. I don't know what your problem is, but you need to start spilling it. Immediately."

He knew she wasn't going to let up, but he thought for once, he could get away with it. Elyse was always one for details. She worked at the speed of light without missing them. At work, it was like she ingested them and you would quickly see the results after her curious appetite was satisfied. He gently placed the pen next to the stack, folded his hands on top of the papers, and briefly looked down before his explanation.

"She deserves another chance."

"Really," Elyse replied sarcastically. "You're kidding me, right?"

"No, I'm not. She deserves another chance to get it right with me. I know it doesn't make sense, and honestly, I don't know why I'm doing it either. But she is owed the opportunity to fix what she broke in me. I can't keep punishing her for it and complaining about it if I never let her prove her words. Remember when we lost the baby last year?"

Elyse could recall every part of the funeral. After all, she was 7-month-old Parker's godmother and was with William when he received the God-awful news. They were shopping for Rachel's birthday present and he was arguing on the phone with her the majority of the day. Along with Parker's little body in the casket, that experience sealed and buried her diminished faith in God. And William, he took it hard. Really hard.

"I didn't act right either. I blamed her for leaving Parker in the car, even though we were arguing on the phone when it happened. I pretended that Rachel didn't exist for an entire month. I didn't touch her. I didn't acknowledge her pain.

I stayed out all night, and when I did come home, I cursed her for murder. I let her suffer twice for our daughter's death, and she let me do it. She forgave me. Elyse, she *forgave* me. The husband that let her absorb the torture of guilt instead of covering her as the rain poured. I'll never forgive myself for that; but, somewhere in that 5'3" frame, her heart was big enough to do what I couldn't. Now, it's my turn. I have to be a husband. I have to forgive her. I'm still pissed as hell that she cheated, but she deserves the chance to make it right. I don't have the stones to throw at her no matter how good it felt to create them."

***

The two sat down at a quaint table, located in the Velvet section of Delilah's, ornamented by a small table lamp and a miniature candy dish. The Velvet section was slightly to the left of the entrance, across from the bar. It wrapped around the outskirts of the bar area and its walls were horizontally halved with burgundy velvet plush fabric, sprinkled with brazen pins as if it were part of a luxurious vintage chaise in its past life. Upon entering the lounge, Malcolm and Elyse sat in the booth facing the stage. No live band was present, but he knew that he didn't want to sit across from her when the band arrived; he looked forward to holding her as they enjoyed the music together. Lena Horne's voice graced the air with sultry ribbons of jazz over the hidden speakers. The glow of the lamp on the table rendered just enough light to view the features of one's face and the desire of one's taste buds on the menu.

"Glad you could join me this evening."

"Glad you invited me," said Elyse, taking her seat.

"So, have you eaten here before you or just sampled the alcohol?" Malcolm jokingly inquired.

"Funny. I've had a few dishes here. The Almond Chicken with Garlic Sauce is good."

"That does sound good." He looked down at the menu to find the details of the entrée. He switched his perusing from the left side of the menu to the right. In his peripheral view, he caught a familiar face across the establishment. She was sitting with another woman and her eyes met his briefly. He smoothly changed his eye line back to his menu and continued the conversation.

"I think I'll try the Stuffed Lobster Tail. What about you?"

"That sounds appetizing. I haven't made up my mind yet," replied Elyse, turning the page. Malcolm sensed that he was being watched. He glanced again past his date and confirmed it was whom he thought.

"Are you okay?" she asked.

"I'm fine. Just drifted in a thought for a minute. I'm back in focus now," he replied with his signature smile.

"That's nice," she replied suspiciously.

Malcolm noticed the woman in the distance and her guest leaving their table. His heartbeat increased slightly when he saw them walking toward his direction. He reached past his glass of wine and took a sip of his water. Elyse could sense someone or something behind her; so, she looked over her shoulder to find a 5'9" latte beauty with big brown eyes standing confidently sweet and smiling brightly at Malcolm. Her shiny waist-length brunette hair reflected the soft lounge lighting like a mirror. She was breathtakingly exotic and Elyse was in awe.

"I thought that was you. How have you been?" inquired the mysterious woman.

"Binnaz. Good to see you again. Elyse, this is Binnaz. Binnaz, Elyse." Elyse extended her hand in polite and silent salutation while her date held his breath in hopes of a positive first encounter. Both women smiled and he let out a silent sigh of relief.

"Nice to meet you." Binnaz reciprocated to her. Turning to Malcolm, Binnaz flashed a smaller smile than the previous one.

"Just wanted to stop by on my way out. It was good to see you again. Take care, Love."

He replied with a simple "Likewise" in hopes that Elyse didn't notice his efforts to stay cool. After patting himself on the back with an imaginary hand, he put an invisible chevron on his sleeve for maneuvering through a possibly awkward moment. Though she noticed that he was taken aback, Elyse was never the intuitive one of the family. That was Shara's gift. Shara could read a person from a distance while Elyse would question them into tears. Currently, she was hungry and anything other than the entrée in front of her was secondary. She noticed that the taste of her dish melted in her mouth and the thyme and rosemary hovered in her nose.

Finding out about Binnaz would have to wait until after she was full.

"How's your food?" she asked him.

"It's great. What about yours?" Malcolm dipped another bite of lobster in melted butter.

"Either it's orgasmic or I was hungrier that I thought."

"I'm going for door number one," he said with assurance.

Elyse shook her head, called him corny, and continued eating. He motioned for her to look towards the stage. When she followed his direction, her eyes lit with excitement. Delilah herself was taking the stage. She was dressed in a red satin ball gown. A gold accessory resembling the branch of a tree was fixed in her curly gray up-do like Christmastime. She cupped the microphone in her hand and began exhaling fluid blue notes. They dripped from her lips like snowflakes catalyzing the audience's attention in mid-air. Everyone knew that she was going to produce a show. Sporadically, she would treat her establishment to the mellifluous sounds of her former Broadway experiences. When she did, it was a special treat and drinks were on the house during her set.

Fly Me To The Moon flowed like silk over the sound system and glasses clinked in celebration. Delilah's eyes shut tightly with soul and the band sailed right along with her into an impromptu jam session. Everyone within ears' distance went along for the ride. Except Malcolm. He couldn't help wondering what business Binnaz had in town.

After the show, Delilah slinked her 72-year-old hips toward the Velvet section to greet Elyse and Malcolm. A beautiful Statue of Black Liberty is who she was. You could tell that she lived a life well enjoyed. Her face was ornamented with high cheekbones and laugh lines around her deep brown eyes. She had iced coffee-colored skin and 4-inch heels that sounded like a symphony of fortitude and wisdom when she strutted around her club. When Delilah was in the room, you noticed. After exchanging pleasantries with Malcolm and Elyse, she inquired about the family.

"How's your daddy doing, Elyse? Is he taking care of himself?"

"Yes, Ma'am. Still losing his shaving cream."

"That man, I tell you. He and your mother sat in this very booth and would fuss about that shaving cream. He was too stubborn to let her win that argument without a fight. And so Ella was a perfect sparring partner for him."

"Yes, Ma'am. She was a perfect match. For all of us."

"Now, don't you go feeling sorry for yourself. Your mother led a full life and she was a gift to us all. Ella was a blessing to the world, Baby. And that blessing lives on through you and your sister. You miss her whenever you feel like it, then you live in that blessing. Live a full life just like she did."

Elyse received the soul of Delilah's message into her heart. She was certain that she would cry if she kept gazing into her eyes, so she consciously looked down at her plate. At least if a tear fell, it would water her plate more than her face.

"Speaking of living full lives, I'm getting everything in place to do that myself. It's finally time for me to sail into my next chapter. Between you and me, I've been taking bids for this old place and I think I've found a buyer that I can trust. Keep your fingers crossed and drink another round on me, Sweethearts."

"But you can't sell it, Ms. Delilah. It won't be the same without you in it. After all, your name is on the building," Malcolm chimed in.

"I can't keep going on like this forever, Honey," she replied. "It's time for me to see the world a bit, go visit some friends, and let someone else worry about the day to day. It will always be mine. I built this place from the ground up, with my blood, sweat, and tears. Nothing can change that history. It's just time to turn the page. We don't stay young forever, Darling." Delilah flipped her silvery bang from her forehead, adjusted her breasts in her bustier, and brushed her hands down the hips of her dress. "Living is not an option, but being stagnant is. Stale water breeds death, Dear. And I don't have time to die on that note."

Elyse's smile was inevitable looking at the legend in front of her. So vibrant and full of herself that she overflowed into everything around her. She only wished that she could be as fearless in her senior years.

"I must say that's some much needed wisdom, Ms. Delilah," said Malcolm. "I admire your confidence and I know your next chapter will be amazing."

"So will yours, Baby." She touched Malcolm's face like an endearing parent. She reminded him so much of his mother.

Delilah then turned to Elyse. "And yours will be too, Sweetie. Remember, no stale water."

Elyse couldn't help but secretly wish that the opportunity would arise for her to purchase the jazz club. It had been tradition to come to Delilah's for New Year's, Monk's Birthday, and just because. She hated to see it fall into the hands of someone who wouldn't understand its precious value. At a young age, her mother and father would speak highly of Delilah's, so much so that Elyse and Shara tried to sneak in at every chance. It was a game of who could portray the most sophisticated lady and neither of them won the host's vote. When Elyse turned 21, Shara and her mother treated her to a night at the famed social establishment – a feminine tradition in their house. It was never a night of over-indulgent inebriation, but a crossing of the threshold into ladyship. Her mother always held the highest standards in terms of her girls acting like young women, which included being able to conduct themselves appropriately at Delilah's first-class yet welcoming atmosphere. Both girls waited anxiously for their "Ladies' Night," just as their grandmother waited for hers back in the 1940s with long white gloves and black heels shining. Women who held the Adams surname could recall their "Ladies' Night" as clear as a fresh glass of water. It was a symbolic gesture that was used to prompt an Adams girl to begin discovering her path in life and sifting through childish inclinations and thoughts. On her special evening, Elyse's mother was illustrious and Shara radiated a similar glow. They were beautiful women with whom Elyse had the pleasure and honor of being seen. She felt like a contest-winning groupie sitting with movie stars, hoping the night would last for hours and praying that she wouldn't make a fool of herself. Though her mother had a sense of humor and that night was the time to let her hair down a bit, she was just too excited that her time had finally arrived. Delilah dedicated a song to her and she shared her first cocktail with the two ladies she admired most. A line of tears arranged single file behind her soul's window panes and proceeded to roll down her cheek as she recollected her mother's smile. Mrs. Adams held that smile until the ovarian cancer aggressively captured her body. It couldn't douse the sweet face her mother had and the fragrant photograph in Elyse's mind. Afraid that assisting with the funeral arrangements would generate too much stress for Shara, Elyse took on as much responsibility as she could hold. Shara was a newlywed and the new principal of a rambunctious middle school. Surely, she would have made the time to handle her mother's affairs, but it wouldn't have hurt to share the load, considering their father was taking his wife's death very hard. His deep grief immobilized him to a silent halt and his daughters worked tirelessly to tie up all of the loose ends. Mrs. Adams, being the meticulous woman that she was, had already made perpetual arrangements – as did Mr. Adams – so their children would have a virtually smooth process. What they didn't include in their planning was the amount of growth the family would experience between the time they purchased their funeral and burial plans to the present—and the Adamses were a close-knit unit. Family members and friends from all over the country flew into town to say their farewells to Mrs. Ella B. Adams, and as with any family gatherings, Cousin Fitz unveiled the video camera to record post-service moments. He thought it was of the highest importance to record the family's growth and experiences. "Every meeting counts," he always reminded them. It was imperative to him that future generations remember the love component of the equation each time they met, whether it was a funeral or wedding. Cousin Fitz got on everyone's nerves with his camera around his neck, but no one turned down his efforts. They knew that he was right. Any moment when family could be together was not to be wasted. Furthermore, every moment was a precious one. Listening to Delilah and the demise of stale water made Elyse want to come clean. She had yet to tell Malcolm that she had been sexually abused in her marriage for fear that the strength she painted before him would disintegrate. But somehow, the frame of that picture wasn't heavy enough to weigh down her need to be free with him. After all, she witnessed the intimacy of bravery to forgive in the most sacred place he held dear and she felt it would be selfish not to do the same. For her, Delilah's was her sanctuary. It was her safety net, and in this moment, it was home. Watching the legend flounce around the room sharing joy with her patrons injected a straightening in Elyse's backbone and she had the courage to walk in that honesty.

"I need to tell you something important and I can't think of a better time than right now."

Malcolm took another sip of his wine and lightly placed the Bordeaux glass on the table. Elyse was an analytical conversationalist, so he knew that being impromptu was just a manifestation of her previous thought processes.

"Please," he affirmed, "Say what's on your mind."

"It's heavy. I'll be lighter once I'm done, but you may not. Is that okay with you?"

"I can handle anything you're carrying, Darling. Nothing you say will change how I feel about you." Malcolm looked past her eyes and rang the doorbell of her heart. "I'm all yours. Go ahead."

His face was comforting and his words were warm. There was something about him that felt like home and Malcolm always made her feel welcome to come into his world. With his reassurance, she gave her heart permission to open the door and told him everything. The fact that she was married when they spent the night together. That her heart felt safe with him when he took care of her after running at the park. The repeated offenses of Kin's sexual aggression. The messy divorce process and how she had to sign an agreement to keep quiet about the abuse.

The more he heard, the faster the rollercoaster around his head travelled. He never believed that extramarital affairs could be justified, but he couldn't seem to hate her need for revenge or affection. There was something about her that made him feel vulnerable and invincible simultaneously. Malcolm monitored his facial expressions to show his focus on her words without causing interruption. The wheels were turning. His palms were glistening with miniature beads of sweat. He had already shared the darkest detail of his childhood and didn't see the need to withhold anything else from her. Like a penitent at a confessional screen, he couldn't deny the overwhelming need to spill his sins to her as well. She seemed to carry the seal of the secrecy and he undoubtedly trusted her. He silenced the murmur and dammed the tidal wave within by finishing the last sip of his wine. He noticed Elyse's hands were clasped on the table, fingers shaking. Malcolm reached across the table and covered her hands. She had unpeeled each layer of comfort she had and he didn't want her to feel alone in her exposure.

"Elyse, I have something to tell you, too. But not here. Not now, but soon. I just have a few things to take care of tonight. I hate to cut our night short, but may I take you home?"

"I...I guess. I wasn't quite ready to go home, but I'll give you some space. I know that was a lot to take in."

I knew I should have saved that conversation for later, she thought.

"No, Beautiful. I meant what I said earlier. I'm all yours. Nothing has changed that." He extended his hand to gentlemanly help her out of the booth. She smiled and placed her lap napkin on the table. Standing carefully and adjusting the skirt of her dress, Elyse replayed her monologue and silently prayed for the best. Malcolm sensed her mind recalling the past hour like a police patrol car looking for clues. He slowly encircled her waist with his arm and kissed her cheek. Before pulling away, he whispered, "I'm not running away, I promise." She saw the truth in his eyes and settled in to it. That smile of his was all she needed to eradicate her fear. Whatever happened the next day couldn't compare to the magic carpet she rode from Delilah's to her doorstep.

CHAPTER 12

"So, what are you going to do?" Elyse asked her sister.

Shara picked up the pouch of hydrangea seeds and put them in her farmer's market basket.

"I'm going with the hydrangeas," she replied. "The lilies will be too passive for the garden. I need something with a bit more punch."

Elyse hated pulling information from her sister. It was like a tooth extraction that took forever, but Shara was the only painless party between the two of them.

"You know what I'm talking about. Stop playing games."

"What do you want me to say? That I'm scared? Hell yeah, I'm scared, Lys. I don't know how to do life by myself anymore. It's always been me and Lenn. Ever since college, he's been there. Now, I don't know where I am inside. My heart feels like a foreign country. I don't know what stories

I'll tell Kaye when the old ones run out. He just told her that he got a job out of town and would be back soon, but Kaye's smart. She's been asking for an address to write him a letter. Not an email address, but a building address so she knows where he is. That little girl has so much sense. I can't tell you how many times her teacher has suggested that we advance her to the 2nd grade. You know, Lenn taught the majority of the lesson plans and I would help her with homework when I got home. At least something worked out right in all of that. I'll see how this whole ordeal affects her Kindergarten year before I make any changes like that. Besides, everything will work out. It has to. I just have to take it one day at a time."

Corn. Okra. Tomatoes. Elyse walked silently next to Shara as she let her thoughts spill from table to table. She had already arranged her work schedule to pick up Kaye twice a week so Shara could conduct faculty meetings, proctor after-school detention, and complete paperwork. She was beginning think that Shara was detaching from the reality that Lenn could be gone for a long time.

"I just want to be sure that you're ready for whatever happens," said Elyse with concern. "I don't want to see you hurt even more."

"Please. If hurt went deeper than this, it would be deadly." Shara picked up a tomato from a local farmer's table and inspected it. "Enough about me. Let's talk about Malcolm and how fabulous he is."

"I don't know about the fabulous part anymore."

"Speak up."

"He cut dinner short the other night after I told him about Kin. I always get swept up in his gentle confidence, but that night, something was different. There was this woman at Delilah's—Binnaz. She was polite, but Malcolm was taken off guard a bit. They have some sort of history. By the looks of it, he hadn't seen her in quite some time and didn't expect to see her again. Her appearance brought up an old memory. I could tell. After my story, he said he had something to share with me too, but didn't want to do it then. I don't know. Something isn't quite right. I want to know, but I don't want to know, which is crazy. What do you think?"

"Does he know that Kin made you sign an agreement that denies cruelty in the marriage?"

"Yes."

Elyse stared ahead as they slowly walked between the rows of tables, which felt more like the middle aisle of judgment in a court of law.

"I see. You want his truth, but you haven't dealt with your own. What are you going to do with the truth once you have it, huh? Are you going to swallow it or throw it up? Those are your only two choices. Digest or vomit. And you better choose wisely, Big Sis, because the truth may be too bitter for you to stomach. You want it right now, but can you handle it? I'll tell you this," Shara paid for the tomato and checked her phone for the time. "There's one problem with the truth that people forget in times like these. It's just like history – it's past tense, legit, and unchanged. No matter how much you think the answer will taste good, the truth is it doesn't. Take it from me. It's molded and grotesque. It may be shrunken and deformed because it's been neglected, but it's still authentic no matter who discovers it. So tell me, what are your plans for the truth? Do you plan to eat all of the food that you're asking for?"

Elyse knew that she had a curious nature that overrode her common sense on most days. As practical as she was, she knew her sister was right. The truth about he and Binnaz may not need to be resurrected. A simple indication of how they knew each other would be respectful, but she knew that he didn't have to tell her anything if he didn't want to do it freely. Now, for putting into practice everything she thought and heard today, that was a baby-step expedition. The first one being forgiving Kin of the spoiled, decrepit bed of truth they wallowed in for six years. Her sister was right. She had to get her ex-husband—and her bitterness—off of her plate.

***

Kin arrived at the house at five past 9:00 PM to gather his mail from the mailbox. He was waiting for an important letter about a piece of property his family owned in Mobile, Alabama and he guessed Elyse would be home soon. After a quick search through the mail, he realized that she may have taken his documents inside if they'd arrived earlier. He reached for his former house key in his suit pocket and walked toward the wrought iron door. Raindrops were starting to drizzle on his blazer and he couldn't twist the key fast enough to duck inside. Kin fumbled with the key and started to feel frustrated.

"I know she didn't change the locks," he muttered to himself.

A few more jiggles of the key and he was convinced that she had done just that. The rain couldn't drown his annoyance, so he decided to wait for her in his car. He marched down the front drive and checked his watch.

9:12.

He instinctively recalled her schedule. It was a Thursday, which meant that she stayed late at work, then headed to the gym. She would be home by 9:20 at the latest. The clickclack of Kin's shoes warned the visitor that the target was drawing near. He quietly stepped out from his hiding place and punched Kin squarely across the eyes. The power behind the fist dismantled his senses and delivered him to the rain-kissed pavement. Kin opened his palm toward the ground to push himself up, but the blows from the visitor consistently landed with precision and brutal force. Blood rushed from his vessels and flooded his skin's outer layer. The raindrops' intensity progressed into a thunderstorm as he accepted the pummeling. Kin's athletic past was no match for the visitor's relentless mission and skill and a gush of crimson escaped from his mouth, diluted on the concrete. His perfectly straight teeth quickly stained with sanguine fluid and the fibers of his white-collared shirt absorbed the trickles that followed the jabs. The visitor ensured his anonymity with black gloves, garb, and plastic molding attached to the bottom of his shoes. Before walking away from an unconscious target, he slipped a note into Kin's suit pocket.

9:15.

Kin looked around to find his attacker gone and his eyesight still blurry. The screaming voice of his pride said that he couldn't let Elyse see him in a beaten state. He couldn't believe what had happened, but the flood lights on the corner of the house shed much-needed perspective as he stood to his feet. He felt paper crumple in his suit pocket when he sat inside his sports car, but didn't recall placing it there. Confused and angry, he reached in and found the following words on a rain-soaked note:

Cruelty begets cruelty. Your honesty is due.

***

"Hello, Darling."

Sitting at Delilah's bar, Malcolm turned his head to find Binnaz standing over his left shoulder. Her British accent always sent a single shiver up his spine.

"Hey you," he replied with his usual coolness.

She smiled and took the seat next to him. She took a sip of his drink and placed the glass on the bar table. Her scrunched face indicated her disdain for his choice of spirit.

"So, why are we here, Dear?" Binnaz asked coyly.

"I should be asking you. What are you doing in town? I thought our assignment was over."

"It was, Darling, but I'm here on particular business. We can't have you slipping around unsupervised."

"I left that life in Turkey."

"Of course you did, but a bit of insurance wouldn't hurt."

"What are you talking about?" Malcolm asked with nonchalance.

"You haven't heard? I'm in the investment business. And this place…" Her eyes looked up and around the bar area in front of her. "…has my best interest at heart."

"YOU are the secret buyer? You must be kidding me," he harshly whispered.

"Perk up, Love. It's just a business deal. Nothing personal. Besides, you left us behind when you moved to America. I'll never know why you chose Birmingham of all places, but such is your decision."

"I chose this city because it's a perfect blend of past and present. Unlike you."

"Awwwww, don't be bitter. Just think of this as a gentle nudge in the right direction. You are our investment, too." Her smile was like a bitter mirror reflecting the foul odor of control that both of them were trained to have under pressure. Malcolm drank the last drop in his glass, placed the empty vessel on the napkin, and looked Binnaz in her honey-brown eyes.

"I told you. I left that life in Turkey. There's nothing here that belongs there. I don't do transfers. You know that. New name. New job…" He paused to ensure that she was listening. "New relationships."

She broke their stare and looked away briefly.

"That was the deal and I've kept my end," he continued. "There's nothing over my head. I'm done and we're good. You can tell that when you report to Mikel."

Binnaz stood up from her bar seat, ego bruised but hidden from view.

"It's been fun, but I've got a business to run."

"I bet you do," Malcolm retorted while motioning to the bartender for the check.

"Take care, Love, and all the best to you and your new çiçek," said Binnaz as she walked away.

"Actually, she's a beautiful çiçek ...*Love*," he punctuated.

***

The smell of the bleached floors mixed with the frigidity of the doctor's office made a nauseous cocktail for Elyse to stomach. It wasn't quite time for her yearly exam, but she decided to move it up a month just to get it over with. Sitting there in that small room with nothing but a sheet for clothing wasn't her ideal item of anticipation. The sooner it could be over, the better. It didn't hurt that all of the staff knew her and her family by name because she had been going there since she was in college. They knew her schedule was demanding and typically worked around it. Elyse returned the favor by sending gift baskets, restaurant gift cards, and thank you notes. It was from the heart, but it definitely made her a favorable patient. She glanced at her toes as she sat waiting for the gynecologist to return and projected a date for a pedicure on her PDA. Her cold feet seemed to make her toenails look unattractive at the moment. She decided to swing them about like Kaye did in her car seat, but heard the door open and stopped the action.

"Elyse. How have you been, Love?"

The voice of Dr. Badasu always brought light to Elyse's face. Her Ghanaian dialect was music to Elyse's and generally made any visit more tolerable. From her jewelry to her hair to her full lips and curvaceous body, she could easily be the envy of any woman and the desire of any man. Not to mention that her vibrant headwraps always ushered joy and life into her office.

"I've been well, thanks! How about you?" Elyse replied.

"Beautiful, thank you. I have the results of your tests here and I've got some news for you."

"Everything's normal and I won't have to see you for 5 years?"

Dr. Badasu smiled charmingly. "No, Love. You still have to grace my presence once a year."

"So what's the news? You know I love good news."

Dr. Badasu smiled again. "Congratulations, Elyse. You're pregnant."

Time stopped and the world reduced to a muffled hum.

"How far along am I?"

She saw the doctor's mouth, but couldn't hear the words. Her lips formed the words *8 weeks* and she made out the term *hCG*, but she couldn't understand anything else.

"I need to be alone."

"Queen, I know this is a bit of a shock, but I really think…"

"I need to be alone, Dr. Badasu," she said with frost.

The doctor's look was a mixture of pity and concern. She knew that the decision would be her patient's prerogative, and she had to respect her wishes. It didn't stop her from putting a nursing assistant on standby near Elyse's door in case she became distraught.

When the door closed, the silence and sterility of the room made the news sink in like a dagger. She knew what she had heard, but her analytical mind couldn't map her next steps. She could only recall the one-night-stand of love and passion at Malcolm's house and the turbulent penetration of Kin's lustful ambition. The counting began. The numbers weren't adding up. The dates for both men did not match the sexual calendar in her mind. The sheer thought of telling her father sent the rest of her sanity down the road of no return. The best decision she could think of was an abortion. It would prevent the embarrassment of the unknown paternity and the truth of her affair. Elyse looked down at her hands atop the clinic gown. Now her hands were the ones that felt dirty. Malcolm's cleansing of the truth came to mind. She was so amazed at how the same hands that engaged in mud were clean enough to hold. Then, without warning, she felt the overwhelming need to pray, to talk to someone higher than herself. It was an abnormal sense that she couldn't ignore. Her eyes leaked with trickles of tears as she began to formulate the words bleeding from her heart.

"I..." Elyse cleared her throat to provide a less obstructed path for her soul to speak.

"I don't know how to start this, but I need your help...God. I was always taught that you were the Father and Jesus was your Son, so I think I'm supposed to pray to you and Jesus will help me." She nervously rubbed her palms together and clasped them in her lap. "This is a pretty serious jam I've gotten myself into. I thought You were always working things out on our behalf and that no weapon formed against us will prosper...at least that's what they say. Well, I don't know where that is supposed to fit. Then again, I guess I can't expect You to save me when I keep picking up the weapon."

The assigned nursing assistant knocked on the door. "Ms. Adams?"

"Another minute please," she requested.

"Are you okay?" he asked, without opening the door.

"I'm praying! Just leave me alone for a minute!"

"Yes, Ma'am," the nursing assistant responded.

She hopped down from the examining table and began to pace the floor.

"I think the problem is I know so much, but I can use so little of it when it comes to You and me. I honestly believe that Jesus is the Son of God and that He died for me on the cross and that He rose from the grave with His own power. My mother taught me that much, but I believe it because I've seen You take care of my family no matter how much we traveled and what crazy situations we experienced. I don't have a problem believing in You, but I just feel too dirty and too far away to ask You for anything. So, let me start with an apology."

Elyse let out a sigh and started the journey she had been avoiding.

"Perhaps I need to ask You for forgiveness before trying to forgive Kin. He hurt me so much, but I guess that's how you feel every day. You made everything around us, yet You can't get a simple *thank you* on most days as we abuse what

You've given us...life. Please forgive me for everything I've done. Forgive me for living like You don't exist...for doing things beneath Your sky that I would never want shown on the big screen. I'm sorry. I need Your help...I need *You*, actually. I've tried to do this my way, but apparently," she paused to look at her belly, "that's not working out too well."

Elyse felt her pride cracking beneath her feet. She had walked on it so long that she didn't realize it had grown so thick, yet as fragile as a semi-frozen lake. The river underneath the ice was intimidating. It suddenly became visible and it scared her deeply. She had not allowed herself to feel out of habit. It was a switch that she eternally flipped downward after her mother's death and the first abusive night of her marriage. There was something about this river of truth that was cold and uninviting, but she had to let the egotistical floor shatter and swallow her into the healing waters beneath.

"Please forgive me for being angry, unforgiving, unfaithful...I don't know how I got here, but I need to come back to You. I know You love me and even though I haven't shown it, I want to love You too. Help me get there. I promise I'll follow."

A light shower of peace drizzled over her head and her breathing slowed. Elyse closed her eyes to drink it in; a refreshing change from the usual tornado within. She opened her eyes and looked at her hands, which had stopped shaking. The floor no longer felt like waves tossing a cruise ship. The Olympic-sized diving pool of emotions now seemed like a pitcher of recycled water that was refreshing her sun-scorched soul.

A few taps on the door from the nursing assistant were followed by a voice.

"Ms. Adams?" inquired the nursing assistant.

"You can come in."

"Dr. Badasu will be with you shortly."

"Thanks. And sorry for yelling earlier."

"It's okay. Sometimes, that's what it takes."

She smiled at his understanding.

"Oh, and amen!" He agreed as he closed the door.

She returned to the examination table and reached for her cell phone to make a call before the doctor arrived, but Dr. Badasu beat her to the punch.

"Hello, Queen. Are you settled now?"

"Yes I am. Wait, why do you ask?"

"Because the entire office could hear your prayer."

Elyse bashfully looked at the art on the wall, then down at her patient gown with a giggle.

"You have nothing to feel embarrassed about here. We've had our fair share of prayers around this place. Daughter…" Dr. Badasu gently held her patient's hand in support. "There are some situations you can jump over and some you must go through. They're either hurdles or tunnels. We would love to have quick jump-overs instead of going through the dark parts of life, but what we don't realize is a track star has to exert faith and energy to clear those hurdles just as the distance runner has to endure dark thoughts from uncertainty and fatigue. God is with you, Elyse. He will help you through this tunnel. You have called out to Him with the rawness of your heart and authenticity is all He requires. Just remember, no matter what, hurdle or tunnel, your Father loves you and He is near. It won't be easy, My Love, but you will never be alone. Today, you walk out of here with your head high knowing that you have a big God and a beautiful village with you. I know it's not what you expected, but you will be just fine." The doctor placed her right hand over their clasped hands for reassurance. "Now, you get dressed and I'll see you soon for your prenatal consultation. The front desk will schedule you." After a few instructions to follow before the appointment, Dr. Badasu's colorful head wrap and the wisdom underneath exited the room.

Feeling good about her new state of mind, body, and spirit, Elyse called Kin to schedule a meeting with him before heading to the front desk. His voicemail prompt began and she left a message with a positive tone. She was sure that he would call her back. After all, it was Monday. As she turned her phone face down next to her, Malcolm's number appeared on the screen. She beamed and quickly answered with a smile that could light a thousand rooms.

"Hello Beautiful," his voice greeted.

"I'm so glad you called. Do you have time to meet tonight?"

"Of course. Is something wrong?"

"No, no. In fact, everything's...right. Surprisingly. I just got some interesting news and I hope it doesn't scare you off, but I need to let you know."

"Elyse, interesting doesn't scare me. I'm interested in everything you are. Whatever you give me, I can handle it. I just hope that my news doesn't scare you tonight either. The conversation I paused at Delilah's? I want to press play on that, if it's okay with you."

"Only if you can live with the results tomorrow," she jabbed.

"Well, let's make it official now...Good Morning."

***

AFTERWORD

Well, here we are. *smile*

First, thank you for reading my outpour. I sincerely hope you enjoyed it.

So often we share the morning and hide the midnight. While this book is inspirational fiction, it was written with this truth in mind.

As Christians, we must stop the hedges of hypocrisy from growing around our lives. They hide the beauty of our humanity and the glory of the cracks in between. A house turns into a home once it has been occupied by living beings. Our struggles and our victories are the spirits that transform this life into an exceptional journey.

Tell the hurting that you have experienced pain as well, that you know how it feels to be scared, broken, and disoriented. Share with one person who feels alone in the sea of despair. The problems of one can be carried by many if we take off the masks and admit that daybreak came after heartache.

Maybe you're the one that is suffocating from the costume of perfection and you don't see a way to receive oxygen. I pray that after this book, you realize that there is nothing too hard for our awesome and magnificent God. He is everywhere at the same time, hearing every prayer.

Start the conversation. It may be a little rocky in the beginning, and that's okay. Keep talking and keep listening. Practice patience and allow the Relationship grow. You'll be glad you did.

Stop by my blog at www.thewritewade.com and let's keep in touch. I look forward to hearing from you and wherever you are, I am praying for you. We're in this together. *Good Morning.*

Peace & thanks for listening,

CJW

Made in the USA
Lexington, KY
30 November 2017